A GENUINE LIFE ENT PRESENTATION

STILL

STUCK

THE MONEY TRAIN

FREDDY SCURRY

GENUINE LIFE ENTERTAINMENT

P.O. BOX

Augusta, GA 33916

ACKNOWLEDGMENTS

First and foremost I will continue to give honor to GOD, whom I'm always seeking first for approval before any move is being made. Without him, I'm nothing!!

To Rosalyn Elaine Pearsey-Murray (my mama!), I love you forever and a day. It's so much I want to bring to the table, I just pray that GOD allows me the time and strength to do so. Thank you for being a praying woman and I'm more than thankful that you never stop encouraging me to push my vision. There isn't a day that goes by that I am not in awe of how you held your family together. You taught me that LOVE is an action word. GOD truly called an angel home when he called you. Rest in Paradise

#PRECIOUSDARLING #GENUINECONVERSATION

Nikki, we've added another beautiful specimen to the family tree! After all the struggles and strife, GOD blessed us with a beautiful daughter, we just so happened to name Patience. I have to admit, she's the most cutest little girl I have ever seen. They can call me bias if they want to, but I'm just being honest. Thank you for being here riding with the family. I know that I'm not the easiest person to get along with, that's just one of the many reasons I LOVE YOU!

Tre and Da'Mon is getting bigger by the day these two cats help me stay focus even when I don't know what being focus is at the time.

Ron, Tamika, Lil John, and Elisha thank ya'll for the love and the support! We get stronger by the day! We all know that mama was a strong warrior for GOD so by far we haven't lost her. When you lose something you don't know where it is. Picture us not knowing where mama at!

Janae, Jamedria, Tameka, and Lil James our time is definitely coming. James Moore, what's up Pops.

To Summer Street, Benning Lane, Hopkins St., Barnes St., Carrie St. and the rest of the 9th Street area, we still making history. To Butler Manor, Barton Village(OWTT), Meadowbrook,

STILL STUCK

Fairington, Southside, Allen Homes, Jennings Homes, Delta Manor, Harrisburg, High and Argon Park, Lake Almstead, Shirley Ave, Glendale, Sunset Villa, Sunset, Old Savannah, Laney, Josey, Glenn Hills, Butler, Hephzibah, Westside, Richmond and the entire Augusta, let's STAND for something. Shout out to the homie/brother Marquail, never underestimate the powers of brotherhood.

To my Fort Myers family, Connie, Dale, Lil Dale, Kevin, Angie, FLEET, Micheal, Jasena, Shannon, Treva, Uncle Reggie, Larry, and Al and Auntie Shirley Jean, Mary Lynn, Odessa, Pat, Cat man ya'll know that I can go on forever..... there is nothing like family!! Rest in Paradise Lamarris and Rapp!!!

I've lived long enough to recognize what's GENUINE and what's fabricated. No more excuses for the people out here just playing a roll to get by. I've thrived on the contents of my character well before I knew the meaning of the words, and I strongly encourage the rest of you to do the same.

Yes, life throws us obstacles, it's how we respond or react to them is what defines us. We've watch how Travon Martin, Mike Brown,

Freddie Gray, Eric Gardner, and Walter Scott MURDERS effect our people as a whole. And these tragedies were recent. I can recall in my city alone how George (Duck) Harvey, Alfaigo Terrell Davis, and Justin (Jed) Elmore were victims to this same epidemic.(R.I.P.) Do we really just suppose go in a corner, pray about it and hope things get better? Who's next? Let's just hope that it's not your child, brother, husband, father or cousin. Kill the shenanigans!

"BEING REAL, JUST AIN'T ENOUGH NO MORE!!"

GENUINE LIFE!!!

PROLOGUE

"Say Weasel, where you?" Jimmy was asking over the phone.

"I'm resting, what up?"

"Man, they just ram-shacked Tom-Tom house this morning! Dude just called me from the county jail!"

Weasel sat up, "What time is it?!"

"Almost ten."

"Bra, you gotta be bullshitting?!"

"Na'll playboy, the feds!" Jimmy replied with aggression, "He say they been watching us for six months."

"He said that shit over the phone?!"

"Just like that!" Jimmy confirmed, "Unk talking real reckless."

"How much his bond?"

"He ain't got one yet."

"We ain't winning with him in there," Weasel revealed.

"I already know," Jimmy acknowledged.

There was a brief moment where it seemed they both were allowing reality to sink in before Jimmy revealed, "Let me jump on this lawyer right fast."

"Make sure you do that!" Weasel stated before hanging up.

Weasel looked over at Ericka, who somewhere during his conversation, managed to sit next to him on the edge of the bed.

She started rubbing his back for a brief moment before asking, "What's wrong baby?"

"It ain't nothing," he replied as he raised up and headed towards the bathroom, "Well nothing that you need to be concerned about, anyway."

"You want breakfast?" She asked as she watched him enter the bathroom rubbing his head.

"Yeah, I could use a good meal right now," he answered.

As he watched her sashay out of the room and toward the kitchen, he couldn't help but shake his head. In his eyes, she was beyond beautiful. He really liked her, which was very rare for him. But with all that said, he knew he still couldn't fully commit to her. For that to be possible, a woman had to be sure of herself, and all of Erica's accessories showed him that she wasn't.

To him, she had all that she needed. Nice figure, cool conversation, topped all of with a pretty smile and a loving spirit. But for some reason, she just insisted on covering her beauty with the fake eyes, nails and hair, so he knew she had no idea of where her true beauty rested. The first sign of being insecure.

The way he looked at it, if Erica was never secure with herself, how could he ever expect her to really feel secure with them?

He knew that in a lot of situations a man could help his woman find that sense of security. But unfortunately, he wasn't holding down that position, nor had the time for such a move, especially with the circumstances he now faced.

As he brushed his teeth and washed his face, he contemplated his next move.

(CHAPTER 1)

"Dam!" Kruger stated through the phone causing Deidra to awaken, "Alright, I'm here bra."

As he sat on the edge of the bed she eased up behind him and wrapped her arms around his chest.

They'd left Savannah in the wee hours of the previous night because he wasn't comfortable with having so much product in that hotel room out of town.

"Is there anything you need me to do?" She asked in a concerned manner.

"Yeah baby-girl," he replied as she started to massage his back, "I need for you to take that bag to the crib. The moment you handle that, call me, because it maybe something else I need you to do."

He smoothly grabbed her hand and eased her around so her head was now resting on his lap. When she looked into his eyes, she could see that he had a lot on his mind.

She knew that her feelings for him were more deeper than his was for her, but she refused to let that hinder her from being everything he needed. In her mind, no-one could ever love him as hard and as openly as she did.

"You know I got you baby," she assured him.

"What's understood doesn't need to be talked about," he replied with a smile of his own, "why you think I keep you around?"

"I just need you to know, regardless of anything, I'm right here," she added with a look of sincerity, "So if there is anything you need me to do, consider it done."

He leaned over and covered her mouth with his. For a moment, it looked as if the time was right, but to his surprise, she broke away.

"I have something I need to do," she announced with a sly grin, "and so do you, so let me up."

"Well, make sure you hurry up and put some clothes on, cause you know how I act when you're around me all naked and shit," he claimed causing her to blush as she made her way to the bathroom.

Right before she reached the bathroom, she turned around and asked, "Do you think we have enough time to take a shower?"

"Start it up and I'll be there in a minute," he replied as he reached in the duffle bag and pulled out a pound of great that he'd got from Firebug.

When he opened the seal on the ziploc bag, the entire room lit up with the aroma. After grabbing a bud he rolled a blunt and had everything back where it belonged before jumping in the shower with her.

"What took you so long?" She asked as she kneeled down in front of him.

The moment she inserted him in her mouth, his eyes rolled to the back of his head before they closed. She massaged his tool intensely with her tongue in such a slow but vigorous manner, that he had to look down at her. After their eyes met he pulled her up.

"Ain't no way!" Was all she heard him say as he picked her up and cradled her thighs in his arms.

Fifteen minutes later they were stepping out of the shower.

"I'll walk you out to the car, just let me fire this here up first," Kruger stressed as he walked over to the nightstand and grabbed the blunt, right before he realized that he didn't have a lighter, "Dam, I forgot to get a lighter."

"I have one in my purse," she acknowledged as she headed for her purse.

"Now what the hell is you doing with a lighter?" He questioned with a disapproving expression.

"I bought it last night when I saw you ain't get one," she stated in her defense.

"I hope you ain't trying to snatch up no bad habits, cause I got enough for the both of us," he implied.

"Of course not, you should already know that," she replied with a smirk, "I'm good with the high that I get off your black ass."

"Yeah, that do sound good."

Thirty minutes later they were walking out of the room towards the elevator. The moment they made it to her car, Hamburger was pulling in the parking lot.

"What up bra?" Kruger greeted.

"What up?" He replied as he stepped out of his truck and embraced him.

"Hey Hamburger," Deidra greeted.

"What up sis?" He replied with a sinister grin.

"Here go the key ole smart ass nigga," Kruger stated as he handed him the card, "I'll be up there in a minute."

"Fool, you can't get mad at me cause I call it how I see it," he joked as he walked away and added, "everybody already know she wifey, ain't that right sis?"

Deidra just laughed it off and kissed Kruger.

"Make sure you call me when you get home," he stressed to her.

She nodded her head in acknowledgement right before Hamburger yelled, "Make sure you tell her you love her too."

Deidra giggled right before Kruger kissed her again and said, "Drive careful and call me when you get home."

"I love you too, Deamon," she stressed with a wide grin as she put the car in reverse.

"Just make sure you call me," he stressed with a broad smile.

Back in the room Kruger and Hamburger smoked on a blunt while they discuss the latest turn of events.

"So what happened?" Kruger asked.

"All I know is they ram-shacked the house this morning and found like two ounces, and they charged everybody in the house with it, including Butler!" Hamburger explained as he sat at the small table.

"Dam, we gotta bond them out!"

"Red might not be able to get out, cause he gonna have a probation hold. He ain't seen his P.O. in a minute," Hamburger revealed.

"What about Black and Rip?"

"You know Black on paper too, but he been on point with his P.O., but with them folks you can never tell. But Rip mama already down there trying to squeeze him out."

"We need to get back at her on that cheese she's about to come off," Kruger stated.

"You know she going to put her house up," Hamburger stressed.

"Well, we gotta get the lawyer or something. It's gonna take a lawyer to get a bond on a trafficking charge."

"What lawyer we going to get?"

"Somebody with some fucking sense!" He answered before adding, "As soon as Deidra hit me up I'm gonna put her on it."

****

"Man, I hope you got something good to tell me," Weasel was saying to Jimmy over the phone.

"Yeah," he replied, "I got in touch with this lawyer and he said that he can have Tom-Tom out tomorrow for 15 grand."

"I know you jumped on that!"

"Yeah, I just sent him ten stacks. I told him that he'll get the other five when he steps out."

"That's all we need to know right there, but I need to get at you on some other shit," Weasel acknowledged.

"Speak up homie," Jimmy encouraged.

"How much bread you working with?"

"No disrespect bra, but we'll discuss all that after this other shit blow over."

"I'm just saying, money still needs to be made," Weasel added.

"And I'm still with you,"

"Cool, hit me when it's time," is all was said before the line went dead.

Weasel sat on Ericka's couch with his eyes on the television. He was glad that Ericka was at work because he had too much on his mind to be distracted. He smiled at the thought of her getting up every morning and going to work, if nothing else, he admired her for that.

After breakfast, a blunt and a few glasses of cognac, the number one thing on his mind was rather or not to eliminate Jimmy with Tom-Tom. On one side he wondered why Jimmy stayed on the phone with Tom-Tom through all that reckless talking, and on the other side, he was thankful for the heads up.

After all his mind boggling, he managed to mumble out one solution, "I remember reading somewhere, that in order for three men to keep a secret, two of them must be dead."

****

Hamburger, Georgia Slim, Big Ox and Kruger sat inside of Kruger's apartment waiting on Tamika to get home from school in Kruger's truck.

"Man, why you ain't tell me that Tamika was pregnant?" Hamburger questioned.

"I did just tell you, fool!" Kruger retorted.

"Well fool, why are you just telling me?" He revised.

"Playboy, I'm just now finding out myself," Kruger clarified with a sincere expression.

"Man, I still can't believe that she pregnant," Georgia Slim claimed before he took a pull from one of the two blunts that circled the room.

"I couldn't believe it either, but believe it playboy, cause it's real!" Kruger assured them.

"Who the baby-daddy?" Big Ox asked.

"Some cat name Keenan."

"You done seen him?" Big Ox interrogated.

"Not yet."

"Time passes by too fast," Georgia Slim implied, "it seem as if it was yesterday she was playing ball for Glenn Hills."

"She 18 now, so you know how that there goes," Kruger replied, "I just gotta show her that big bra is here for her regardless."

"All of her brothers!" Hamburger stressed as he passed Kruger the blunt.

A few moments later Tamika walked through the front door and the first person to say something to her was Big Ox.

"Girl, why you ain't tell me that your pregnant?" He practically snapped.

Tamika just looked him up and down before she stressed, "Sit your ass down!"

All of the other fellas burst out laughing as Tamika put her book bag and purse on the couch and stated, "Ya'll got it smoked out like no other in here."

"My bad," Kruger stressed, "open these windows and that sliding door so it can air out in here."

"Yeah, cause she don't need to be inhaling this smoke," Georgia Slim added.

"Do you have somewhere you need to go?" Kruger asked her.

"Na'll, but I need some money for my senior pictures."

"How much you need?"

"One-fifty."

Tamika wore a wide grin as she watched all of the fellas dig in their pockets and pull their money out, "Thank ya'll," she stressed as they all handed her fifty dollars apiece.

"You just make sure that you let Teresa know that I'll be back around six," Kruger told her as him and the fellas made their way out the door.

Five minutes later they all was piled in the truck and headed towards Summer Street.

"Say playboy, what did wifey say about the lawyer?" Hamburger was asking Kruger from the passenger seat.

Kruger just gave him a grim look before stressing, "Deidra, said she hired some dude, but I forget his name."

"Did he get them a bond yet?" Big Ox asked.

"She said that he ain't gonna be able to get them a bond until tomorrow sometime, so they all have to at least sit for the night."

"I talked to Rip's mama and she stressing the same thing," Georgia Slim revealed.

"They good though, cause me and Burger took them some boxers and shit up there earlier," Kruger stressed.

"I bet the Summer is booming right now," Big Ox spat out, "and ain't nobody got nothing."

"Well, we'll ride through and see what's up, cause we don't need to get trapped on a humbug," Kruger stated before pausing for a moment and adding, "if shit straight, then ya'll can get straight right now."

"I've already told you what I want," Hamburger announced with a wide grin.

"With you smiling like that, you must about to cope you a brick?" Georgia Slim inquired.

"Now there you go trying to check my pockets," he replied after turning around to face him.

"Yeah, that's what he about to get," Big Ox assured with a sly grin of his own.

"Nigga, how you know what I'm about to do?" Hamburger questioned.

"Cause you got the same look on your face that Bad-Azz had when he coped his first brick," Big Ox replied.

"You know too dam much!" Hamburger spat out with a wide grin as he turned back around in his seat.

"I try not to let too much get by me," Big Ox replied with a sinister grin.

"Nigga, what the hell are you about to spend?" Kruger sarcastically questioned as he looked at Big Ox through the rear view mirror.

"I got nine fool," he replied, "so whatever you gonna let a playa get for that."

"Dam Slim," Kruger stressed as he looked over at him, "I know you ain't let Ox pass you like that?"

"I told you what was up the last time I coped, ain't nothing changed since then but the news and weather!" Georgia Slim retorted.

"My bad bra," Kruger replied, "so it's still official, Ox is still the one on the Summer with the least amount of bread," he added causing all of the fellas to burst out laughing.

"Hell na'll!" Big Ox retorted, "Ya'll must forgot about Pimp."

"Pimp don't count, he's hardly ever on the Summer," Hamburger pointed out.

"He been trying to get right," Big Ox stressed in his defense, "I'm surprised that he wasn't in the house when it got busted."

"He must have came to his senses and realized that nobody looks out for your pockets, like you," Kruger stressed as he pulled in Gurley's parking lot.

"Speak of the devil," Hamburger stressed as he saw Pimp walking towards them from the porch.

"What's up Mr. Kruger?" Pimp greeted as he stepped out of the truck.

"Cooling playboy, what's good with you?"

"Shit, just catching these few sales. I didn't know what ya'll was gonna do, so I coped a few ounces from Ugly-O on Carrie."

"I see you ain't playing," Kruger pointed out as they started walking towards 1122.

"It's time out for playing," he replied before asking, "but what's the word on the fellas?"

"They at least gotta sit the night but they should see a better day in the morning," Kruger replied.

"Have them folks been riding?" Georgia Slim asked him.

"Man, ain't nothing been through here but a few weight sales and a whole bunch of fiends," Pimp replied with a sly grin.

"So, everything been everything?" Kruger asked.

"Yeah playboy," he replied with a sly grin, "they too funny ain't gonna fuck with us, not after catching that lick this morning."

"Oh yeah?" Kruger replied with a quizzical expression as he took a spot on the porch with the rest of the fellas.

"Somebody must have let them in, cause they ain't bust the door down or nothing," Kruger added after seeing the door untouched.

"Now that's something you gotta ask them," Pimp implied.

After looking up and down the street Kruger stressed, "Well, everything look good to me, but it's on ya'll."

"Nigga, we waiting on you!" Hamburger retorted.

Without uttering another word Kruger grabbed his phone and headed towards the middle room. A few moments later he was on the phone with Deidra.

"What's up baby-girl?" He greeted.

"You," she replied.

"I need you to bring three, and pull up at Dyess Park. When you get there call me."

"I'm on my way," she replied before the line went dead.

When he walked back out to the porch he told the fellas to give him thirty minutes. He then made his way towards Gunslanga's house, before Pimp yelled for him.

"Yeah, what up?"

"A nigga need some work," Pimp stressed as he caught up with him.

"You gotta walk and talk playboy, cause I gotta check on this broad down here," he replied as he started back up the sidewalk before asking, "what you working with?"

"I got five stacks."

"I gotcha playboy, but I need the whole five for the quarter," he implied before adding, "I usually tax the fellas 45, but you know they been fucking with a playa, and this just your first time."

"Dam playboy!" He retorted.

"That's the best I can do," he responded, "but every time you ree-up I'll drop a hundred off until you make it to 45."

"I guess I can work with that."

"Nigga, you're gonna at least bring back 13, so I know it ain't nothing," Kruger blasted, "you ain't buying it hard, cause I ain't serving it to you like that."

"That's what's up!" He responded with a wide grin.

When they finally reached Gunslanga's trap the first person they saw was Vader on the porch.

"Kruger, what the hell are you doing walking around with that one arm freak?" Vader questioned with a sly grin on his face and a crack stem in his hand.

"If I was you I'll mind my business, before I collect them 50 dollars you owe me off your ass," Pimp stressed to him before walking in the house behind Kruger.

"I take it that you're ready to ree-up?" Kruger asked Kay-Kay who was lounging on the couch.

She looked up at him, then at Pimp and rolled her eyes, "I still got like two left, but Prime gave me that other stack for Slanga," she added as she raised from the couch towards her room with Kruger right behind her.

After walking in the room behind her and closing the door, he asked, "How much you working with?"

"Eight and some change," she replied as she grabbed the money from under the mattress.

He just glared at her as if she had lost her mind. He wanted to ask her what she was doing with her money, but he knew it wasn't his place, so instead he asked, "So what you trying to spend?"

"Probably eighty-five hundred, if I was to get something right now."

"I guess I can shoot you like 350 grams for that little bit, but I should only give your ass 300!"

"See, why you tripping like that?" She questioned, "You don't see the fact that I'm down here by myself."

Kruger thought to himself how he would love to have the spot all to himself, but she obviously looked at it differently, so he just told her, "I'll see if one of the fellas would come down here with you tonight."

"Why can't you stay, you already know that you owe me," she pleaded.

"I gotcha," he stated as his phone rung, "you just gotta be patient."

"What up?" He answered after grabbing his phone.

"I'm here," Deidra replied.

"I'll be there in a second," he replied before pausing for a moment and adding, "matter of fact, get out and go to the swings."

"Alright," she replied before hanging up.

"I'll be back in like ten or fifteen minutes," he stressed to Kay-Kay as he walked out of the room.

As he walked through the house he told Pimp the same thing. When he reached the porch he told Vader to come with him.

"You gonna stop trying to tell me what to do," Vader protested as he raised out of his seat.

It didn't take them no time to reached the swing set in the park where Deidra was waiting patiently with a duffle bag laced over her back.

"Dam gorgeous, who the hell is you?" Vader excitedly asked before pausing for a second and adding, "The things I could do with you."

"Chill out Vader, before I do something to you," Kruger stated before kissing her on the cheek.

She took the bag off and handed it to Kruger before saying, "I have you something to smoke in there too."

Kruger handed Vader the bag and said, "I need you to go sit on them bleachers with this, while I talk to her for a second."

Vader started walking before he turned around and said, "I don't care if you beat my ass, but that's a fine ass woman you holding down."

"Man, go ahead and let me holler at her for a minute," he responded with a wide grin.

"Baby, he's crazy," Deidra stated while blushing.

"Yeah, but he good peoples."

"He gotta be, if you trust him to walk with that."

"Yeah, right."

"But what's up with you, Mr. Kruger?" She asked with a broad smile.

"Nothing really," he replied, "I just wanted to thank you for being who you are to me."

"Come here," she demanded as she pulled him closer by his shirt.

"What do you want with me?" He asked playfully.

She wrapped her arms around his neck and eased her tongue deep into his mouth. He responded immediately. After a few moments he pulled away from her.

"I'm gonna stop by when I'm through with this," he stated as he licked his lips.

"You make sure you do that," she replied as they parted.

He watched as she sashayed to her car and couldn't help but feel proud.

"I'll be waiting," she yelled as she made it to her car.

"Alright baby, I'm on my way!" Vader yelled back from the bleachers.

The moment Kruger was in arm distance of him, he slapped him across his head and said, "Now didn't Pimp just tell you about minding your own!"

"You must ain't heard what I told him?"

"What did you tell him?" Kruger asked with a devilish expression.

Vader looked over at Kruger and burst out laughing before stressing, "Do I look that stupid? You actually think I'm gonna tell you that?"

Moments later they were walking back in the house with Pimp and Kay-Kay.

"Say Kay-Kay, where that big scale at?" Kruger asked after snatching the duffle bag from Vader.

"Now, all you had to do was ask for it and I would've gave it to you," Vader stated with a sincere expression.

"Man we too dirty to be playing games, so get out there and watch the street!" Kruger practically ordered.

Without another word Vader made his way to the porch while Kruger grabbed one of the packages and unwrapped it. It had to have

34

been the most cocaine that Pimp had ever seen because his eyes were now as big as golf balls. Pimp watched as Kruger broke the hard powdery substance into smaller portions and placed them on the scale.

"Dam, that shit looks as if it's been cooked already," Pimp stressed.

Kruger just looked over at him with a smile before saying, "Welcome to the other side of the game."

After placing 250 grams on the scale he told Pimp, "That's you right there, and it should be some Ziploc bags in the kitchen drawer."

After he finished his business with Pimp, he went through the same process with Kay-Kay. Ten minutes later him, Pimp and Vader were walking back up Summer toward 1122.

"I appreciate that homie," Pimp mentioned to Kruger as they walked in the middle of the street while Vader walked on the sidewalk with the bag.

"You the one who's been prolonging, so thank yourself," Kruger replied.

"You definitely ain't gotta worry about that no more," Pimp assured.

"I hope not," Kruger replied with a little aggression.

"I feel where you're coming from bra, but just give me a minute and you'll see."

The remainder of the walk to 1122 was a quiet one. When they reached the porch the door was locked so Kruger had to bam on it.

"Who is it?" Big Ox finally asked through the door.

"I'm dirty playboy!" Kruger stressed.

"My bad bra, we off in here playing the game," he revealed as he opened the door.

"You good," Kruger assured him as him and Vader made their way to the middle room.

Vader quickly handed him the bag and made his way back to the porch. Kruger opened the bag and grabbed another package and handed it to Hamburger. After snatching it from him he walked out of the room with a wide grin.

"Do I need to break this in half, or can ya'll handle it?" He asked Georgia Slim and Big Ox as he pulled out another one.

"You know I wanted a quarter with mine," Georgia Slim reminded him.

He then dug in his bag and pulled out the remainder of the package he had broke down for Pimp and Kay-Kay and handed it to him and said, "That's like 400 grams or maybe a little more, so I'm gonna need twenty-three more dollars on that, but you can get that at me when you get straight."

Twenty minutes after making sure everyone was good, he pulled out heading for Deidra's house, blasting Trick Daddy's, *"Hold On"*.

****

"What do you mean, you don't know?!" Surina was yelling at Jimmy as she stood over him in their hotel suite.

"Just like I said!" He retorted as he looked up at her from the bed, "I don't know!"

"We done been in this room for two days straight!" She snapped, "You don't want me to go nowhere or nothing, and when I ask you how long we have to be in here, all you can tell me is that you don't know! Wrong fucking answer, Jimmy Kliene, wrong fucking answer!"

"Why you tripping?" He questioned as he sat up, "You act as if we've been here for weeks or something. We haven't even been here three days yet."

"I'm just saying, I had plans to go out tonight with Ericka, but we can't go cause ya'll muthafuckas gotta lay low. I can't believe all of us suffering cause ya'll fucking with ole lame ass Tom-Tom!"

"Listen Surina, if you wanna go out, ain't nobody stopping you. I already got enough shit on my plate to be dealing with that bullshit you stressing."

"Who the hell you talking to like that?!" She questioned with aggression.

Jimmy stood up and replied, "You know what, you're an inconsiderate rachet ass bitch! I should've been left your trifling ass alone. Now, I feel what Weasel was stressing. You probably did hit me for that quarter, and if I find out you did, I'm gonna let loose all type of fire in your ass!"

She just gazed at him with a shock expression. Jimmy had always kept a cool and calm manner when dealing with her, so she was totally caught off guard.

"So you don't trust me because some shit your boy done said?" Was the only thing she could conjure up, "Let me tell you something muthafucka! See, you think Weasel your friend, but that nigga don't give a fuck about you. If he did, he'd be his ass over here with you, instead of hiding out at Ericka's house!"

"What the fuck is you saying?!" He retorted.

"Why you think that Deamon them don't fuck with him like that too funny, huh? Cause he's shady as hell and can't be trusted!"

"Hell, they say the same thing about you!" He revealed.

"Nigga, whatever! All I know is that I ain't in no position to fuck you over, so why keep your eyes on me?"

"You're just talking out of the side of your head," he stressed as he walked in the bathroom.

"Yeah, I can see that you're getting heated," she stated as she grabbed her purse and headed towards the door, "and I'll appreciate it if you forget my number, cause when the Feds get your ass, I can't afford the collect calls."

"You act as if you're telling me something I don't know already!" He stated as he walked back in the room, "That's why Kruger don't fuck with you, because you're a selfish, inconsiderate and disloyal bitch!"

"You don't know shit about me and Deamon!" She spat out as she turned around and faced him.

"I know that you took him to T.G.I. Fridays a couple of months ago," he revealed while observing her shocked expression, "yeah I know. I also know that to him you ain't shit, and them niggas really frown on me for fucking with you."

"What?!" She managed to say, "Fuck that!" She added as she walked out the room slamming the door behind her.

Jimmy heard a loud thud and rushed to the door. After opening the door, he noticed her balled up on the floor crying her eyes out.

"Dam baby-girl," he stated as he grabbed her and carried her back in the room, placing her on the bed.

-TERESA-

"Deamon, where have you been?" I asked the moment he stepped through the door.

Yeah, he called me and told me that he'll be a little late, but ten o'clock, just ain't gonna cut it.

"Dam, Mrs. Elaine Craig," he had the nerve to say causing Tamika to burst out laughing.

Me and her was watching, '*Waiting To Exhale*', when he walked in smelling like weed mixed with some other woman, so I really didn't think that his remark was funny at all.

"I thought you said that you'll be a little late?" I questioned as I stood up to look him in his eye.

"I guess this is the part where you slap me and tell me that I don't need to be coming in this time of the night," he replied as he moved his face in a good position so I can get a good hit.

Lord knows I wanted to knock him senseless, but I refrained from the physical and gave him the verbal, "Stop playing with me Deamon!"

The way I see it, me and him has a lifetime ahead of us, so if I allow him to play me stupid now, things would only get worse.

"You ain't serious," he replied as he lifted my extra large t-shirt to see what I had on under it.

I stepped away from him and stressed, "Don't touch me!"

"Oh you can't be touched now?" He snapped back, "I don't see you all week and when I do finally come home, you don't even ask me how I'm doing. I thought we talked about this."

"I did too!" I replied, because it was no way I was going to allow him to put me in a corner like that, "If I can remember, we agreed that you'll be more considerate about us. So nigga, you knew I had beef before you even walked through the door."

"Can we talk about this a little later, because I would hate to get shined on in front of my little sister," he asked in a playful manner.

He's always trying to pull this stunt, but since I really missed him, I just shook my head,

"Whatever, but let it be known that I'm telling you you're gonna fuck around and make me fuck you up."

"So, I can't get no hug or nothing?" He asked with that sly ass grin that I love to hate.

"Do you think you deserve a hug?" I cross examined.

Do you know this fool just walks passed me towards the room and said, "You know, it shouldn't matter what I think."

He must have knew that I was coming right behind him, because he went straight to that bottle on the side of the bed.

"I hope you coming back here to give me that hug and ask me how my trip was?" He implied.

"I guess I can do that much, since I see that you're already stressed out about something."

"Does this mean I can get a back massage too?" He had the nerve to ask.

I wanted to curse him out, but I knew that I would be only pushing him closer to whoever he just left, so I compromised instead.

"This is your lucky night," I stated as I walked towards the door, "I'm gonna run your bath water and let you soak for a minute. And after I bath you, I'm gonna give you a full body massage."

"What, you're trying to spoil me or something?" He asked with a light smile.

"I just think that I need to start giving you a reason to come home on time," I implied as I walked out of the room and into the bathroom.

Sometimes I think I love this dude too much. Yeah, I can admit that I may smother him from time to time, but dam, I hardly ever get to spend time with him. It's like I'm competing against the streets. And from my experience with David, if that what it is, I know that I'm in a no win situation.

I mean how can you compete with a man's passion? It makes me wonder, who he really belongs to, me or the streets.

Truth be told, I know that he's out there with other women, because David did the same shit. Yeah, I wanna ask his ass about it, but I also don't want to put him in a position where he feels he needs to lie to me. To some that might sound ignorant, but fuck them. Besides, I'm only speculating.

I guess that's why I'm in here running his bath water, cause I need to remind him that the good stuff is right here. So, if another woman even attempts to seduce my man, he would at least think twice about what he has at home.

(CHAPTER 2)

"Say Weasel," Jimmy was saying through the receiver, "Tom-Tom just got out!"

"Where he at now?" Weasel asked.

"Probably on his way to the house."

"Come scoop me, so we can figure out how we gonna handle this."

"Give me an hour."

"I'll be here," Weasel replied before he hung the phone up.

Ericka was asleep next to him when he rolled out of bed, so he gave her a light shove to wake her up. After she rolled over to face him he asked, "Why didn't you go to work?"

"I told you I was taking the day off so I can pay some bills," she yawned out.

46

"You ain't tell me that," he responded as he lightly slapped her naked thigh.

"Stop!" she yelled out, "You must got somebody coming over here?"

"Na'll, but I'm about to ride out with Jimmy for a few," he replied with a sly grin as he made his way out of bed and headed towards the bathroom.

She raised up with an attitude, "But I wanted us to spend the day together!"

"We can get together a little later, but right now I got something to take care of," he replied as he grabbed his toothbrush and toothpaste.

"That's cool," she replied in a not so understanding manner, "just as long as you don't forget about me."

"Now, tell me how am I gonna forget about that fat ass?"

She blushed as she made her way to the bathroom before she asked him, "Do you have time to eat breakfast?"

"Anything but pork," he stated in an agitated manner, "I'm trying to leave that swine alone."

"I wish you would've told me that yesterday, I would've bought some steaks or something."

"Well, you know now," he stated as toothpaste ran down his chin.

"You so nasty!" She interjected as she sashayed out of the bathroom.

"Don't you think you need to turn around and hit this toothpaste?" He replied after rinsing his mouth.

"Don't try to shine, cause I had to remind you all week to hit that toothbrush," she rebutted as she made her way back to the bathroom, "for a minute there I thought you was scared of it or something."

"Would you please stop talking," he chuckled as he placed his hand over his nose, "and brush that little Viking out of your mouth."

She lightly struck him on the arm and stressed, "Alright now, that's enough!"

"I told you that I was gonna get your ass back," he reminded her as he walked out of the bathroom with a wide grin.

"Say Ericka," he added as he grabbed her hair extensions off the bed, "don't put this shit back in your head."

"What shit?" She asked as she peeked her head out of the bathroom.

He threw the extensions by the bathroom door, "That shit!"

"Stop tripping," she replied as she rolled her eyes at him, "and you talking about me."

"I'm dead serious," he declared as he grabbed the half of blunt he'd put out the night before and sparked it up.

After he took a long pull and exhaled he added, "You look straight without it, you don't need that extra shit. If you can't grow it or wasn't born with it, you don't need it."

"You ain't said nothing about it when you met me," she responded as she walked out of the bathroom and stood in front of him with her hands on her hips.

"We wasn't fucking like we're fucking now, either!" He informed her before he took another pull and added, "You were suppose to be nothing more than some hit action. But now it has advanced to something more."

She was silent for a moment and he could tell that she was caught off guard, so he attempted to ease things a little.

"You know that I ain't trying to run you or nothing, it's just that when you're out there, you have to know that you're representing me. Dam near everybody in Augusta know we kicking it."

"I can feel that, but you gotta know that goes both ways," she proclaimed as she walked out of the room.

He then took another long pull of the blunt before he called her name.

"What do you want now, daddy?" She yelled from the kitchen.

"Come here right quick," he stated as he dug in the night-stand drawer.

The moment she stepped to the door she asked, "Now what you called me back for this time? What, you wanna tell me that you don't like my feet now?"

"Girl, come here!" He demanded as he waved a fistful of money at her.

After she stepped to his side he said, "This is like 350. I want you to go and get your hair done in an original style. Get your nails done too, but your nails, not none of that press on shit, and take them contacts out."

"Why can't you accept me for who I am?" She whined out in a dreary manner.

"I'm trying to accept you for who you are," he replied as he pulled her into his lap, "that's why I'm telling you to kill all the accessories."

She looked at him hard for a moment before she finally asked him, "You don't want me?"

"If I didn't want you, I wouldn't bother to let you know that I care how you look. You're the one who must don't want to be with me?"

"You already know I do," she replied with a sincere expression.

"So stop tripping and act like it," he stated right before he passionately kissed her.

After a few moments she pushed him away with a wide grin and said, "Now, that we have that settled, let me fix us something to eat.

STILL STUCK

****

The sounds of Kruger's cell phone ranging woke him up. The clock on the nightstand read 11:47am, and he found himself in bed alone.

"Good morning boo, I hope I didn't wake you," Teresa said after he answered.

"Something like that, but I'm good. What's good with you though?"

"You, I just called to let you know how much I enjoyed your company last night," she stated with a joyful attitude.

"Oh yeah."

"Of course," she replied before adding, "Did you get my little note I left on the pillow with the rose?"

He looked over next to him and noticed the rose with the letter under it before he playfully asked, "Now, what if I would've rolled over and got stuck by one of those thorns?"

"And you're welcomed," she giggled, "with your ungrateful ass."

"You know that I'm just tripping," he replied with a wide grin that she couldn't see.

"You're not gonna read the note?" She asked.

"Yeah, I'm gonna read it."

"So, what are you waiting on?"

"It says, Deamon, thank-you for last night, it was truly special. It was a refreshing reminder of why I continue to believe in us. I hope you know that I'm looking forward to waking up next to you for the rest of my life."

"You like it baby?" She finally asked him after a brief moment of silence.

"Yeah, that was straight right there," he managed to reply.

"You know that I'm dead serious about that rest of my life thing?" She implied with a sincere tone.

"Do you really think that you can handle me, Ms. Thang?" He replied.

"Of course, or I wouldn't even be bothered with your ass."

"That's what your mouth say."

"Na'll baby, that's what I know!" She retorted causing him to really smile.

"I thought you couldn't talk on the phone at work?" He asked in an attempt to rush her off the phone.

"I can't, but I had to talk to you!" She excitedly replied.

"Well, stop putting your job at risk and call me when you can."

"Alright boo, I'll call you later."

"Do that."

"I love you."

"Yeah, right."

"Bye Deamon."

"Bye, Ms. Thang," he replied before hanging up.

After sitting up, he grabbed the blunt that he'd left over from the previous night and fired it up. He then walked in the living room to the sound system. After pushing a few buttons the sounds of *So Real* by UGK blasted through the speakers.

"I ALWAYS WANTED TO BE THE BIG MAN IN SOMETHING, HAD TO FIND MY PLACE," is what he heard the rapper Bun-B recite as he relaxed on the couch.

****

"Weasel!" Ericka called from the front window, "Jimmy downstairs blowing the horn."

A few moments later he was walking through the living room when she pulled him by the arm and stressed, "Now I know you wasn't about to walk out of here without showing me some love."

He then wrapped his arms around her and gave her a passionate kiss. When he finally pulled away from her he said, "Just remember what I told you to do today."

"Yes daddy," she replied.

"Well, I'll see you later."

"Alright baby, just be careful out there," she stated as she pulled him back and stole another kiss.

Moments later he was in the passenger seat of Jimmy's Q-45 heading towards Tom-Tom's house.

"So what's the plan?" Jimmy asked with a worrisome expression.

"It ain't really no plan," he replied before taking a pull of the blunt Jimmy was already smoking, "we just gotta take the bastard out. The nigga has violated every code that I stand for!"

"I'm understanding all that," Jimmy assured him, "but we don't know who's in the house with him."

"Listen playboy," Weasel stressed with a gruesome expression, "I frankly don't give a dam if the pope was in there with this fool, off with his muthafuckin head too!"

"So be it," Jimmy spat out.

Weasel could sense that Jimmy still wasn't feeling the situation, "Look bra, I know this really ain't your field, but if you have another way to handle this dude, I'm listening."

"I'm straight homie, just pass me that bottle from the backseat," he replied with beads of sweat appearing on his face.

Weasel reached in the backseat and grabbed the bottle of gin and handed it to him before saying, "I need you in your right mind, so don't hit this shit too hard."

The rest of the ride was silent. Neither said anything until they reached Tom-Tom's neighborhood.

"I don't think that we should pull in his driveway," Jimmy stressed before taking another gulp of the gin.

"You right," Weasel agreed, "we might need to park down the street and go through the backyard or something."

After passing Tom-Tom's house, Weasel spotted an abandoned house a few houses down from Tom-Tom's. The top of the 'Century 21' sign read open house, "Pull up in there," he motioned.

Jimmy followed his directions and parked the car in the driveway.

"Now, I'm gonna go through the backyard since there isn't nothing but woods back there," Weasel implied, "I'll hit the fence why you walk up and knock on the front door."

"Why can't I go through the back with you?" Jimmy questioned.

"Cause I need you to knock on the front door to take attention from the backyard."

Moments later Jimmy was walking down the street towards Tom-Tom's house, while Weasel was jumping the fence of the abandoned house. Weasel was determined to get to the house before Jimmy knocked on the door, so he made sure that he moved at a faster pace.

In the backyard Tom-Tom had an old '69 sky blue Bel-Air, that was parked next to an old shed that had weeds growing over the small steps.

When Weasel stepped towards the bedroom window, he could hear Tom-Tom singing in the shower. His first thought was to walk around and let Jimmy know where Tom-Tom was until he noticed the window slightly opened, so he quickly snatched the screen off and raised the window up.

He didn't know how long he was going to be in the shower, so he was moving as quickly as he could. By the time he was through the window he heard the doorbell.

Tom-Tom obviously couldn't hear it over the shower, because he was now singing louder.

Weasel just smiled at the ordeal as he fixed the blinds and curtains back the way they were, before heading to the front door. As he walked through the house he had to maneuver between lamps and clothes that was just thrown every where from the police searching for evidence.

When he finally opened the door he had his index finger over his lips before saying, "Be quiet, he in the shower."

Jimmy walked in and grabbed his pistol from the seams of his jeans before Weasel pulled his arm and said, "Slow down playboy, you moving too fast."

"What up?" Jimmy asked with a bewildered expression.

"What I need you to do is sit on his bed and wait for him to come out of the shower," he added.

"Just as soon as he come out, I'm gonna pop his ass!" Jimmy stressed as he made his way towards the master bedroom.

"Na'll playboy!" Weasel spat out as he grabbed his arm again, "Just don't let him get out the tub until I get back."

"Where you going?" He asked with an confused expression.

"I'm just going to clean up the little mess I made in the backyard," he responded as he made his way towards the sliding door.

Before he made his way to the door he grab the dish rag from the kitchen sink. He grabbed it and used it as a glove to open the sliding door. After making it to the window he'd climbed through, he wiped the window off where he felt he'd touched it and placed the screen back in. That was around the same time he heard the water from the shower stop.

Inside Jimmy was sitting on the edge of Tom-Tom's bed with his 9mm clutched tightly in his grasp and pointed directly at the naked man. So the moment he pulled the shower curtain back, the first thing he saw was Jimmy and the pistol.

"What the fuck!" Tom-Tom stuttered out.

"Don't muthafucking move, you soft ass son of a bitch!" Jimmy slurred out as he raised up and stepped towards him.

"Dam, what's this all about?" He asked in a pleading manner, "Whatever it is, we can take care of it, we ain't gotta go this route."

Weasel walked in around this time and threw Tom-Tom a towel, "Wrap that around you."

"Can't I at least dry the fuck off before I catch a cold?" Tom-Tom questioned..

"Believe me playboy, catching a cold is the least of your worries!" Weasel revealed, "Now if you don't tell me what I need to know, you bound to catch a few slugs from ole Jim-bo here."

"What the fuck brought this here to the table?" He questioned, "I mean haven't I showed you both love?"

"First off," Weasel stressed, "we ask the questions and you answer them. Now step out and follow me."

"Now, don't try anything stupid!" Jimmy stated with a gruesome expression.

Tom-Tom walked out of his room behind Weasel with Jimmy right on his trail. When they reached the living room, Weasel instructed him to have a seat on the couch.

"I want you to know that me and Jimmy don't like the fact that you talking all reckless on the phone after you got busted," he started to say before pausing for a moment to observe Tom-Tom's reaction, "Now, you know they record that shit and for all we know you was standing right next to the police when you was talking to Jimmy."

"Na'll Weasel!" Tom-Tom started to plea before Jimmy cut him off.

"Na'll!" He snapped as he pointed the pistol to Tom-Tom's head, "Nigga, no matter how you look at it, you folded! I mean who really talks like that from the police station! And you OG?!"

Tom-Tom was spellbound. He never thought that he would ever be in the position with these two. He had never saw Jimmy this hysterical and Weasel so much in charge.

"Na'll man, that's not what went down!" He retorted with his hands up toward Jimmy who now had the nose of the pistol pressed against his temple.

Weasel now wore a sly grin, "I think it's best you just keep quiet, cause anything you say can leave you with an body full of holes."

Tom-Tom dropped his head and nodded, knowing what Weasel had said was true.

"Now, what I wanna know is where the rest of the dope and money at?" Weasel questioned as he winked his eye.

"I ain't," he started to protest before Weasel waved him off.

"Now the thing is, I'm only gonna asked tha t questioned once!" He asserted as the smile disappeared from his face, "Now keep in mind, if you don't have anything to offer, how can you pay us back for all the trouble you've caused these last few days?"

Tom-Tom looked over at Jimmy, then up at Weasel before replying with, "Everything I got is buried in the backyard, everything else is in the street."

"So you telling me that if I look in that old shed in the backyard or check that old Chevy, I won't find anything?" He interrogated in a calm manner.

"I should have like fifty grand stashed in the gas line of the Bel-Air," he answered in defeat.

"So, how was you gonna pull that out?" He investigated.

"I can get it out," he replied.

"Take him to the back and let him put on some clothes," Weasel instructed Jimmy.

"You heard him old rat muthafucka!" Jimmy stressed.

While Jimmy followed Tom-Tom back into his room Weasel took a seat on the couch. He was contemplating on whether or not it was wise to take Jimmy out at this point.

At first he thought that Jimmy would fold, but now he was seeing a different side of him. He knew that the gin had a lot to do with his demeanor, but to him, regardless of what was making him handle the situation, he was handling it like a pro. The way he saw it, if Jimmy was willing to pull the trigger, why should he stand in his way.

"Ya'll really need to hurry up in there!" He yelled down the hall.

A couple of seconds later they were walking towards him.

"Now, the first thing we're gonna do is snatch that little change from the car, then we can snatch that little bit from the other spot," he insisted as he rose from his seat.

"I'm good with that," Jimmy replied, "and this muthafucka here, has no other choice but to be good with it too."

The three of them walked out the sliding door towards the Bel-Air. When they reached the rear of the car, Tom-Tom pulled the old license plate down, twisted the fuel cap off and started to pull up a piece of wire that was barley noticeably sticking out.

"Now are ya'll happy?" He asked after pulling out the full wire which contained rolls and rolls of bills.

"Hell na'll, we ain't happy!" Jimmy snapped, "Nigga, I have more than that in my niece's trust fund and she ain't but seven."

After they all jumped the small fence and walked about twenty feet away, Tom-Tom picked up a shovel that was laying next to a tree, and started to dig right behind it.

A few minutes later he'd found what he was looking for. When he reached out to grab the old leather tote bag, Weasel slapped him across the back of his head with the .45 and grabbed the bag.

After Tom-Tom let out a deep groan, Jimmy stepped up to him and put the 9mm to his head and squeezed the trigger twice. The sound of the gun blast echoed through the woods as he stood over the body.

"Let's go!" Weasel demanded as he pulled him away.

Jimmy started to go back towards the house, but Weasel instructed him to go through the woods towards the open house. As Jimmy followed his instruction, Weasel grabbed the shovel and started to erase their foot prints.

After erasing their foot prints, he stopped to look at what was left of the man who'd helped turn him into a five figure hustler.

****

"Say baby," Deidra was saying to Kruger as they stood in the kitchen of a townhouse in downtown Augusta, "I don't too funny like how this one is built."

"Me either," he replied before pausing for a moment and adding, "I like the little condo in Columbia County better."

"Besides," she added, "it's too close to 9ᵗʰ street."

"And you know that I'm definitely not feeling that," he revealed as he made his way toward the front door, "and it ain't no way that I can survive resting this close to the Summer."

"Dam baby, you're not gonna wait for me?" She asked as she stood behind him with her hands on her hips.

He turned around with a wide grin, walked over to her and picked her up as if he was carrying her over the threshold.

"So, I guess this means that we're married now?" She sarcastically implied before she pecked him on his cheek.

"I guess it does," he replied as he carried her out the door and to her car.

The manager of the apartment building walked over to the car as they were settling in and asked, "I take it that the townhouse wasn't appealing to you?"

"No mamm, it wasn't," Deidra replied with a warm smile.

"Well, I'm sorry about that, but I do wish you two the best of luck on finding a place that suits you," she stated with a genuine smile before pausing for a moment and adding, "might I add that you two look wonderful together."

"Thank you Miss," Deidra responded as she looked over at Kruger who just shrugged his shoulders.

"No, I'm the one who should be thanking you!" She retorted, "I'm blessed just to be able to see young couples enjoying each other's company the way you two do. You see, it's so many couples out here fussing and fighting these days, it's a shame. But it looks like you both have that special someone in your life, so make sure you hold on to each other."

Deidra just blushed before she cranked her car up and replied with, "Well, thank you again Miss, and have a nice day."

As Deidra pulled off, Kruger looked back at the lady, who was still standing there with a wide grin on her face.

"She was real sincere about that," Deidra implied as she placed her *Erykah Badu* cd in the disc player.

"Yeah she was," Kruger agreed as he sat back in his seat, "but she spoke some true shit.

You could tell that she done lost someone she really loved."

"Deamon, you should be a counselor or something, cause you think you can diagnose everything," she implied.

He just looked over at her and smiled before saying, "There was a lot of things I could've been, but I was always up to know good."

"You sitting there talking like you're already dead or something, what about now?" She asked as she stopped at the red light, "I mean what do you wanna be now?"

He looked out of the passenger window for a moment as if he was contemplating the question before looking back at her and placing his hand over her stomach before he replied with, "To be honest with you, I don't even think that far ahead no more. I just wanna be comfortable out here and watch our seed grow."

His response made her smile, but he could tell that she wanted to say more on the issue.

"Go ahead and say what's on your mind, baby-girl," he encouraged.

"You know that you can't be in the streets all of your life, unless you plan on being locked up or dead in a minute. You have to find something else to do."

He took his hand off her stomach and looked out the passenger window again before replying, "I can feel where you're coming from, but shit just ain't that sweet right now."

"That's the main reason you should try to venture off into something else, cause you know it ain't that sweet out here," she stressed as the light turned green.

He looked over at her before leaning over and kissing her on the cheek, "I guess I should be thinking about that a little more often."

"I know you love me," she blushed, "you ain't never gotta tell me."

He just shook his head and smiled as *Erykah* chanted the fact that she would see him next lifetime. After a few moments of listening to her he asked, "So, what time did the that lawyer say he'll have the fellas a bond?"

"He should have it all set by now," she replied.

"Well, we need to be heading down that way to see if we can snatch them up or something."

"My friend in booking said that if they have a hold on them she'll camouflage things to make it seem as if they don't."

"Dam, that's right on time!" He excitedly responded.

"I thought I told you that?" She question with a sly grin.

"You know you ain't tell me that!" He retorted.

She lightly giggled before saying, "It must have slipped my mind or something."

****

Jimmy and Weasel sat on the couch in the living room of Ericka's apartment with dope and money all over the coffee table.

"Dam playboy, I'm proud of you for stepping up to the plate like that," Weasel stated.

"Nigga, I told you that I could handle it," he replied before turning up the bottle of gin.

"Yeah, but I thought that you were going to choke up."

"To tell you the truth, I thought I was too," he confessed allowing them both to get a laugh in.

After they both regained their composure Jimmy looked at the table and said, "I always thought that the dude was worth more than this here, cause three bricks ain't shit."

"Nigga, you got a brick and a half and twenty-five stacks for an hour of work, think about it like that, and you'll always come out on top," Weasel pointed out as he raised from the couch towards the bedroom.

"Bra, believe me I ain't complaining," he responded with a sly grin.

Jimmy sat there with his bottle in hand and just stared at it for a moment. He was obviously marinating on the earlier events, because he looked as if he was spaced out. He had that same crazy expression on his face when Weasel walked back in the living room.

"You alright playboy?" He finally asked after standing over him for a moment.

"Huh, oh yeah, I'm good," he managed to stutter out, "I was just thinking about how that fool was looking after I put that hot lead in his dome."

"Check this playboy, before you get to acting all crazy and shit!" Weasel stressed as he took a seat next to him, "You ain't no killer! The only reason you pulled this here off is, you ain't had no choice."

"Now where the hell did that come from?" He asked in a confused manner after seeing the gruesome expression Weasel wore on his face.

"You have that same little smirk I had when I caught my first muthafucka," he implied before adding, "you have to know that pulling the trigger is the easiest thing to do, but trying to rest at night is where shit gets difficult."

"I'm good playboy," he insisted, "I mean I have no regrets for what just went down."

"When you wake up screaming and hollering with the bed as wet as a pool from you sweating, don't call me!" He snapped back, "Hell, I have my own demons to deal with."

"I can respect that," he replied with a sly grin, "but it sounds to me as if you're the one that's spook."

"You'll soon understand," Weasel assured him as he raised from the couch and walked in the kitchen, "just remember to keep your mouth shut!"

✱✱✱✱✱✱✱✱✱✱✱✱✱✱

Kruger sat on Deidra's porch talking on the phone with Gunslanga. He could sense that Gunslanga was growing tired of being away from his natural habitat. He attempted to ensure his comrade that he wasn't missing much, but he knew he was speaking in vain.

So changing the conversation was all Kruger could come up with, "Hell, I'm thinking about heading down the way myself and pulling an all nighter."

"Now you know Teresa ain't going for that!" Gunslanga stressed after bursting out laughing, "Fool, you done been gone all week, and now you think that your ass gonna stay away from the house tonight. Playboy, you're gonna fuck around and make her lay hands on you."

Kruger just chuckled before replying, "I admit, you do have a point."

"Go home playboy," Gunslanga insisted, "that way she can't trip when you really need to dip."

"True that, but check this out my folk," Kruger stated as he sat up right in the chair, "I'm sitting here on Deidra's porch and the old man just pulled up."

"And?"

"You know he always asking about you when I'm over here."

"What he be saying?"

"Nothing really, but hold on," Kruger stated as he dropped the phone from his mouth to speak to Deidra's dad.

"How you doing Mr.McNeil?"

"I'm alright for now," he replied in a nonchalant manner, "have you been staying out of trouble?"

"I have to if I wanna stay free," Kruger replied with a sly grin.

"Have you talked to Mr. Frazier lately?" He asked while walking through the front door.

"Na'll, not lately."

"Well, when you talked to him, cause I know you're gonna talk to him soon," he stated as he stopped in the doorway, "let him know that he can't run forever."

The way the detective sounded and was looking, Kruger could've sworn that he knew Gunslanga was the one on the phone with.

"Did you hear that?" Kruger asked after the detective went in and closed the door.

"Yeah, I heard him."

"The nigga hit me with the same shit, dam near everytime he see me."

"Dam him, he'll be alright," Gunslanga stressed before adding, "well I'm about to raise off this horn, but hit me up if something goes down."

"You do the same."

"Much love playboy!" Gunslanga stressed.

"Til death!" Kruger replied before pushing the end button.

Kruger sat there for a moment and thought about the comments that Deidra's dad had made and it irked him. He knew that to most people he was looked down on, because of the way he made a living. He never let it get the best of him, because the way he looked at it, there wasn't a man alive perfect. The way he felt, just like they judged him, they were being judged by GOD. So that was basically how he handled it, he let go and let GOD.

"You ready to go baby?" Deidra asked as she stepped out the door.

"I'm ready if you're ready," he replied.

"You alright," she asked with concern, "why you looking like that?"

"I'm good," he replied as he raised from his seat, "I was just thinking about something."

"Well, do you mind if we stop by your mama's house, cause my daddy told me to drop this casserole dish off," she implied as they walked towards her car.

"Yeah, we can do that," he responded with a light smile, "I wanna see my little brothers anyway."

"Me too," she agreed as they got in the car, "that Benny Jr. know he crazy."

"Yeah, the little nigga is wild as hell," he agreed before asking, "they must have had one of them outings at church?"

"I think so."

"Hell, those were the only times I use to like going to church. It's like it was easier to sit through all the yelling and screaming when you have a fat plate waiting for you in the back," he mentioned causing her to burst out laughing.

"You are nothing but the devil!" She managed to giggle out as she pulled out of the driveway.

"You know I'm far from that, I'm just trying to tell you how it is. They use to drag us every Sunday morning to get ready for Sunday School."

"You talk as if you didn't like Sunday School?"

"It all depended on who was teaching that morning. If they had somebody young who a playa could relate to, it was cool. But a lot of the times they didn't have no-one, so they would get that same deacon's wife, and you know I wasn't trying to hear nothing she was saying," he replied in a sincere manner causing her to burst out laughing again.

Moments later they were pulling in Kruger's mother's driveway. His baby brother, Lil Man was playing basketball at the end of the drive way, but when he finally saw Kruger, he threw the ball down and ran towards him.

"What's up Deamon, where you been?" He asked as he jumped in his arms.

"This woman had kidnapped me for a minute," Kruger replied as he picked him and pointed at Deidra.

She was already at the front door when she heard what he said, "I ain't about to let you put that on me!" She stressed as she pushed the doorbell.

Kruger just smiled at her as he put Lil Man down.

"Man, I done got too big for you to be picking me up," Lil Man stated with a wide grin.

"So that means that you think you can beat me now?" Kruger asked as he picked the basketball up.

"Yeah, I can beat you!" He replied as he followed him to the goal, "You know that them new Jordan's come out in the morning?"

"What, you want them?"

"Man, you already know!" He retorted.

"Well, you know you gotta be up early in the morning."

"Why can't I just stay the night with you, we ain't got no school tomorrow," he implied in a pleading manner.

"You gotta ask mama."

Without another word spoken he ran in the house past Lil Benny who was coming out the door.

"I'm about to ask mama can I stay the night with Deamon so I can get them new J's in the morning!" He stressed to Lil Benny.

"I'm going too!" Lil Benny stated as he followed his baby brother.

Kruger walked in the house behind them both and yelled, "Hey in here!"

"Boy come in here and hug your mama!" His mother yelled from the kitchen.

"What up mama?!" He greeted as he walked up and embraced her.

"Boy, you getting big, what you been eating?" She implied as she let him go.

"Nothing really," he replied with a smile.

"Well, I'll hate to see you after you ate something!" She responded as she went back to cutting up an onion, "So they going with you?"

"Yes mamm."

Lil Man ran to the back without saying a word, while Lil Benny tried to act cool and walk behind him and yell, "Boy, you know mama don't play you running through her house!"

He then turned around and said, "Now, if that was me, you'll be whipping me all up and down this hallway."

"Boy, it's best you get somewhere before I knock you senseless!" She told him.

"You see what I go through?" Lil Benny implied as he looked over at Kruger and Deidra before walking to the back room.

Kruger and Deidra just burst out laughing right along with his mother before she said, "That boy is gonna make me hurt him."

"Yeah he do be tripping, don't he?" Kruger implied as he walked towards the stove to check the pots.

"Boy, I wish you would touch my pots with them nasty hands!" His mother yelled, "If I don't bust you across your head, my name ain't Elaine Craig!"

"It ain't Craig, it's Pearsey, and don't you ever forget that." Is all Kruger replied with as he made his way next to Deidra.

"Deidra, tell me you don't handle your daddy like they be trying to handle me?" Kruger's mother questioned.

"No mamm," she shyly giggled out.

"So where the preacher at?" Kruger asked.

"He had to run to the church, he'll be back in a minute."

"Well, we ain't got time to wait, we got a few things to take care of," Kruger revealed.

"What ya'll about to do?" She curiously asked.

"Now there you go all in mine," he replied with a sly grin as he walked towards the front door.

"Now, how do you manage to put up with that?" She asked Deidra.

"I guess you just learn to love it after a while," she replied as she followed her man.

"Ya'll better hurry up if ya'll coming," Kruger yelled down the hall before he brought his attention back to his mother and asked, "you need some money?"

"You gonna give me some?" She questioned.

"And you wonder where I get my attitude from," he replied with a broad smile as he handed her a few hundred and kissed her on the cheek before saying, "I'll talk to you a little later."

"Make sure you take care of my babies," she stressed as they all walked out of the house.

STILL STUCK

****

Tamika sat in 401 Walton Way's parking lot waiting on the fellas to exit. When she pulled up, her watch had read 4:27pm and now it was reading 5:10pm and they still hadn't made their way out the tall building. She had already reclined the seat to get comfortable for the wait, so every five minutes or so she'd peek over the dash board to see if they were coming.

"Open this door girl!" Red stated after knocking on the window.

"Nigga, you scared the hell out of me!" She snapped back while hitting the button to unlock the doors.

He jumped in the back with a wide grin before asking, "Where bra at?"

"I don't know," she replied as she threw her phone to him, "call him and see."

"Dam, you balling out of control now, you got you a fly ass phone and all," he stated as he dialed Kruger's number.

"Where the rest of them at?" She asked in an impatient manner.

84

"They should be coming out in a minute," he replied.

After hearing Kruger's voice he asked, "Where you at bra?"

"What up playboy, when they set ya'll free?"

"Just now, you know it takes them folks decades to process you out."

"True, but I'm at the bowling alley on Gordon Highway."

"We should be up there in a minute," he replied as Black, Rip and Butler walked out the county jail doors.

****

"Deamon, you want me to go and get you something to drink?" Deidra was asking while stringing up her bowling shoes.

"Na'll baby-girl, I'm good right now," he replied before looking over at his brothers and asking, "ya'll want something?"

"Yeah, I want a beer," Lil Benny replied.

85

"Boy, you ain't old enough to drink no beer!" Lil Man stressed before looking over at Kruger and implying, "Is he, Deamon?"

"He know that he ain't old enough to be drinking no beer," Kruger confirmed with a light smile.

"That's why mama say that she don't like taking him nowhere, cause he don't know how to act!" Lil Man revealed.

"Shut up nigga!" Lil Benny stressed with an attitude.

"Ya'll chill out and head over there with Deidra while I put our names in the computer," Kruger stated as he waved them away.

"Ya'll come on, cause he tripping right now," Deidra instructed them as she rolled her eyes at Kruger.

Kruger couldn't help but smile as he watch her with his brothers. He was loving how she smiled to the way she walked. To him she was beautiful, but most importantly, she was loyal.

Lil Man was starting the third frame when Tamika and the fellas walked in.

"What up playboy?" Red greeted as he walked up to Lil Man.

"What up Red?" He replied as he dapped him up.

Kruger walked over and embraced them all before looking over at Tamika and saying, "Finish my game while I holler at the fellas for a minute."

He looked over at Deidra, who was now giving him a cold stare, and said, "I ain't about to go nowhere."

Butler started complaining about he wanted something to eat, so Kruger handed him a fifty dollar bill and he went straight to the concession area.

"So what's the status on ya'll pockets?" Kruger asked them as they walked towards the bar area.

"I'm still straight," Rip assured, "they didn't get nothing but two hundred jacks from me."

"All I lost was like four-fifty and an onion," Black added.

Kruger nodded his head before looking over at Red and asked, "So what up with you?"

"I lost a little bit, but I'm straight," Red stressed with a sly grin, "I'm just mad at the fact that I gotta cope my first brick three days behind schedule."

"What you mean, three?" Kruger chuckled out, "you was only locked up two."

"I know, but I promised that broad Kim from booking that I was gonna holler at her," he replied with a golden smile.

"That ain't a bad idea playboy, cause she sounds like she good people," Kruger encouraged before looking over at Rip and Black and asking, "So what ya'll gonna do?"

"We might as well crank up in the morning too," Rip agreed, "cause you know I have to check in with mom-dukes anyway, you know she been running around taking care of everything for a playa."

"Yeah, I might as well do the same," Black agreed.

Kruger nodded his head before implying, "Ya'll just make sure you get at me first thing, cause I have to be out and about all day."

✳✳✳✳✳✳✳✳✳✳✳✳✳✳

Jimmy was stretched out on the bed in his hotel room fast asleep before he was awaken by a hard knock at the door. He looked over at the digital clock on the night-stand and saw that it read 4:25am.

"Who is it?" He reluctantly asked as he crawled out of bed with his pistol in hand.

"It's me, Jimmy," the familiar voice replied.

After opening the door and seeing Surina there dressed in a khaki ¾ length coat and high heels on, he said, "I thought you said you didn't like being in here with me?"

"I never said that!" She retorted as she walked past him into the room, "what I said was, I hate being trapped in here like I was some kind of fugitive."

"It's five o'clock in the morning," he stated as he closed the door and jumped back in the bed, "how did you know that I didn't have company?"

"Because you're my man, and you know better," she replied with a seductive smile as she undressed in front of him, "Now aren't you gonna ask me what I'm doing out at five in the morning?" She added as she continued her minor strip tease.

"To be real with you, it ain't really my business," he replied in a nonchalant manner, "besides, if you wanted me to know, you'll tell me."

At first his remark stun her, but she brushed it off and continued as if she didn't hear a word he'd just said.

"I'm sorry about our little altercation," she stated as she climbed over him, "do you think that there is anyway I can make it up to you?"

"I could think of plenty ways," he replied with a straight face, "but neither could be done all in a day, let alone a night."

"Baby, I'm willing to spend a lifetime making it up to you, if that's what it takes," she assured as she kissed him lightly on the lips and traveled to his neck and chest before asking, "do you have a problem with me starting right now?"

(CHAPTER 3)

"Say Red," Kruger was saying as they smoked on a blunt on their way to *Zaxby's* on Walton Way, "I see you and ole girl Kim are getting pretty close."

"A little something like that," he replied with a sly grin, "hell, I'll be a fool not to in my position."

"I can feel that, cause she definitely an ace in hole with your probation situation."

"Yeah, but you looked out too homie," he stressed as he passed him the blunt.

"You my peoples, so all I did was play my position," he replied before taking a long pull of the blunt.

"That's why I have so much love for you bra. It's hard to find those traits in a nigga out here."

"That's why we don't fuck with just any nigga out here," Kruger replied with a cloud a smoke seeping from his nose and mouth, "as long as we stick together, can't nothing hold us, just as long as we don't fold bra. I just wish Bad-Azz and Hammah was out here to help contribute."

"Yeah, I miss them niggas too," Red agreed with a light smile, "you know Bad-Azz would be flossing hard as hell right now."

"And me and Hammah would be tripping off that cat, thinking he Scarface and shit," he added before they both burst out laughing.

"You know," Red stressed as they both regained their composure, "I've been out for almost two weeks and you know that I've been grinding my ass off. But I still ain't getting money as quick as you and that nigga Slanga did."

Kruger sensed that Red was a little frustrated so he stressed, "Man, all I remember was being out there with that monitor on and telling myself that I wasn't going nowhere until I at least had eight stacks, everything else is a blur."

"So, what you trying to tell me to do is grind harder?"

Kruger passed him the blunt before asking, "You remember on the first when all those weight sales came through and ya'll sent them down to me?"

"Yeah."

"Why you ain't serve them cats?"

"I was trying to get a bigger profit."

"Now, remember ya'll got popped with those two onions?"

"How could I forget?"

"Now, how many weight sales did ya'll turn down that day?"

"It was a few," he replied as Kruger pulled in *Zaxby's* parking-lot.

"Now, what I'm stressing is we got plenty of dope. You're working with a brick so kill that nickel and dime shit. You can serve that shit how you want to and still come out with a nice cushion. It's all about the quick flip.

When I serve ya'll, I really ain't making no profit," he added, "but a nigga going through the dope so fast that it doesn't matter. As long as I know that there is more where that came from, I sell that shit for the low every chance I get."

Red and Kruger had a nice history together. They went back as far as coping fifty packs together, so as Kruger spoke he had his ears wide open. There was never any animosity in the air when it came down to them. If one was slipping, in any area, it was the others duty to put him point.

"You right playboy," he agreed as they both exited the truck.

"You can't lose like that," Kruger assured as he opened the restaurant door for Red.

As they walked in they noticed that despite it being busy, all eyes were on them.

"Welcome to *Zaxby's*, can I take your order sir?" The female behind the counter asked Red.

"Yeah," he replied as he looked over at the white manager who seemed to be standing over her, "I wouldn't mind enjoying a large wings and things combo, with tongue torch wings and bar-b-que sauce instead of that *Zaxby* sauce."

"Will that be all sir?"

"No mamm, I want a strawberry soda and rang up whatever he want on my order to," he added as he pointed toward Kruger.

94

"And what would you be having sir?" She asked Kruger.

"The same thing the same way," he replied.

"Will that be all sir?"

"Yeah that's it," he replied as his phone rang.

"What up playboy?" The familiar voice greeted him through the receiver.

"Shit, just chilling right now," he replied as he walked out the restaurant.

"I need to get at you."

"Well, I'm at *Zaxby's* on Walton Way."

"Well, order me a wings and things combo, large, I should be there in a minute."

"Alright playboy, I got you," he stated before pushing the end button and walking back in the restaurant where Red was sitting on the waiting bench talking on the phone.

"I wonder who it is you're on the phone with?" He implied as he walked past him and toward the counter.

"Yes sir, can I help you?" The same girl walked back to the register and asked.

"Yeah," he replied with a sly grin, "I'm gonna need another wings and things combo, and make them all for here please."

"You must be real hungry?" She inquired as she rung the order up.

"Na'll, it's just somebody else joining us," he replied as he handed her the money.

"I hope it's not your girlfriend?" He heard her imply.

"Na'll, it ain't her," he replied as he appraised her.

"So, if I give you my number are you gonna call me?" She asked.

He just smiled at her before replying with, "If you would've caught me a few months ago, I would've had no problem with that, but I refuse to put you in the mix of this crazy situation I find myself waking up to every morning."

"How old are you?"

"Twenty-one."

"You talk as if you're thirty or forty years old. Hell, I'm older than you!"

"Oh yeah," he replied with a smirk.

"Yeah, and it wasn't like I was trying to marry your young ass, I just wanted to see where your mind was at."

"What did you say your name was?" He asked as he leaned on the counter.

"I never did," she replied with a smirk of her own.

"Well, my name is Deamon, what's yours?"

"Phylisha," she replied as she pointed at her name tag.

"How old are you Phylisha?"

"I'm twenty-five."

"That just goes to show you that age doesn't mean a dam thing," he stated as he stood back up.

"What are you trying to say?" She asked with an attitude.

"I mean all you want a playa to do is swing through when the kids are sleep and smoke and drink a little with you, and eventually tap that ass," he stated in an irritated manner, "You don't want a nigga who is gonna be there and make sure the fridge is tight or the bills are paid on time. You want a nigga who's just looking for a good time."

"You don't even know me!"

"I know, but I see your kind every time I go somewhere," he assured her as he dug in his pocket and peeled off a twenty dollar bill and handed it to her.

"What's this for?" She asked openly confused.

"That's so you can get the kids something to eat when you get off, cause I know that they are tired of eating *Zaxby's*," he stated before walking off and sitting next to Red who just happen to still be on the phone.

Kruger couldn't believe how shallow minded the lady was. He knew that he could have got with her later and sexed her without even trying. He thought he was doing her a favor, but when it all boiled down, she felt offended. He knew that he had made the right decision by leaving her alone, because the way he looked at it, if she was that thirsty for company, there was no telling what she'll do to hold on to it, and he definitely didn't need that heat.

"You alright playboy?" Weasel asked after sneaking up on him.

"What up my folk?" He replied as he stood up to embrace him, "Is everything good with you?"

After seeing Kruger raise up to greet Weasel, Red followed suit.

"Dam playboy, I forgot to order your drink," Kruger implied.

"I got it playboy," Weasel replied as he headed towards the counter.

"Hey Weasel," Phylisha greeted him with a wide grin.

"What up Lisha, I ain't know that you was working here," he replied.

"I've been here for almost two months now. You know I gotta pay the bills for now, and I refuse to start stripping at *Dolls*."

"True," he responded with an understandable head nod, "but how Mark doing?"

"He good, you know I'm gonna keep him straight if nothing else."

"I see you trying to get thick on me, what's up with that?" He implied with a smile of approval as he continued to appraise her.

She just blushed before finally implying, "You must have forgot my number or something?"

"Na'll, I still got it, I mean unless you done changed it or something? I really just been knee deep in a lot of bullshit lately."

"Well, I get off at six, make sure you get at me," she replied with a seductive smile.

"Will do, but while you're up here, why don't you grab me a strawberry soda."

"Say Weasel," Kruger called out, "see if you can grab ours while you're up there."

Weasel watched as Kruger and Red walked to a table in the far right of the restaurant before turning to her and saying, "See if you can get my people's drinks too."

"You know I'll do anything for you."

"You still smoking?" He asked as he eyed the way her *Dickies* were fitting.

"You know it," she replied with an approving grin after seeing his eyes focused on her ass.

"Well, I'm gonna swing through with a bottle or something, you know how we do it," he stated as she handed him a tray with their drinks on it.

"You already know that I'm down, you're the one who's been missing in action."

"I'll make up for it," he replied before heading to the table with Red and Kruger.

"When ya'll food gets ready I'll bring it over," she stated causing Weasel to stop for a moment and give her a head nod.

"I see that you've found your future wifey," Kruger stated with a sly grin.

"Nigga, you know that we ain't in the business of turning hoes into housewives," is what he managed to chuckle out.

"I thought you might be slipping on a playa."

"My nigga, I might slip from time to time, but believe me, I ain't slipping like that!" He firmly stressed as he took a seat across from him.

"I guess that's good news."

"Yeah, whatever, but on some other shit, you know that Tom-Tom's body was found yesterday," he informed him with a serious expression.

"I heard, but Deidra told me that her daddy them frustrated cause they don't have no leads on the case."

"That's good to know," Weasel replied as if he could finally exhale.

"Just stay on point, cause you know they still can come holler at ya'll," Kruger instructed.

"I can feel that," Weasel replied before changing the conversation, "but I need to holler at you about some good prices."

"What you looking for?"

"Well, I was coping like two from ole boy for twenty-four a piece, so if you can match that, I'm good," he replied.

"I tell you what," Kruger stressed as he pondered over the figures, "I need this one cat checked, so if you can handle that for me, I can let you get them for twenty-three a piece."

"Holler at ya boy," he excitedly replied.

"This the dude that's got Slanga in the cross right now and all I need you to do is take him to 401 to fill out a statement, get a copy of the statement and give him twenty-five hundred for me."

"That's it?" He asked openly disappointed.

"Yeah, that's it."

"When did you need that done?"

"Like yesterday."

"That's cool, cause that's about the same time I needed to get straight."

"My nigga," Kruger replied with a broad smile, "you can get straight right now."

"And I'll take care of that first thing in the morning."

"Bet that," Kruger stated as he raised from his seat, "I'll be right back."

He walked outside and sat in his truck before he called Deidra.

"Hello," she answered.

"Baby-girl, I need like two of them things."

"Hey, how you doing?" She sarcastically replied.

"My bad, how you doing Ms. Sexy?"

"I'm alright," she replied with a light giggle, "where you at?"

"Walton Way, just hit me up when you get this way."

"Where on Walton Way?"

"At Burger King."

"Alright boo, just give me like twenty minutes," she stated before the line went dead.

When he stepped back in the restaurant Red was off the phone and Phylisha was bringing their food to the table.

"Are ya'll alright?" She asked while standing over Weasel.

"You straight, Kruger?" Weasel asked him.

"Kruger?" Phylisha responded as if she'd heard his name before, "I thought you said your name was Deamon."

"Would it have mattered?" Kruger asked with a smirk.

"I guess not," she responded before walking away.

Weasel watched her as she walked away before looking over at Kruger and asking, "Now what was all that about?"

"It was just another case of looking for love in all the wrong places."

They were halfway through eating when Kruger's phone rang.

"Yeah, what up?" He answered.

"I'm here," Deidra replied.

"Hey, how you doing?" He responded with a sinister grin.

"I knew that you was gonna do that," she giggled out.

"I'll be there in a second," he stated before pushing the end button.

He rose from his seat and looked over at Weasel and said, "Have that ready, I'll be back in five."

A few moments later he was pulling in Burger King's parking-lot next to Deidra's Honda. She stepped out of the car and jumped in his passenger seat with a duffle bag.

"Why didn't you bring me anything from *Zaxby's*?" She asked with a sly grin of her own.

He just smirked before responding, "I didn't do that because of you, I did it because I don't want everybody in our business."

She leaned over and kissed him softly before saying, "I just wanted you to know that you can't hide from me."

He then reached over and passionately kissed her. For a moment she was overwhelmed, but she eventually regained her composure and pushed him away.

"I need you to handle your business," she stated with a lustful expression, "after you take care of that, you need to come and take care of me!"

"You know I love it when you try to act all hard," he stated as he placed the bag between their seats.

She just smiled before getting out and walking around to the driver's window.

"I'm about to go and get us a room, I'll call you and let you know the room number," she revealed before kissing him again.

He watched as she pulled off before he himself did the same. When he reached *Zaxby's*, Red was back on the phone and Weasel was in a deep conversation with Phylisha.

"I guess your manager didn't like when me and my homeboy stepped in here earlier, huh?" Kruger asked her.

"It wouldn't have mattered, now would it?" She retorted with a sly grin before she rolled her eyes and walked away.

Weasel watched in illusion as she walked away without saying another word before he looked back at Kruger and asked, "Did ya'll use to fuck around or something?"

"Probably in another lifetime," he replied as he headed towards his truck.

Weasel handed him a *Zaxby's* bag and said, "That's forty-six right there."

Kruger handed him the duffle bag without saying a word.

After looking in the bag he looked back up at Kruger with a wide grin before asking, "Now how am I suppose to get in touch with this Buck dude?"

****

Gunslanga laid on the couch of Teresa's old apartment with Amanda asleep on his chest. They'd just had a heated argument about him laying low, well at least to him, she did. He already knew what he needed to do, and that was to leave his temporary cell immediately.

Being in that apartment made him feel like he was still behind those prison walls. The way he looked at it, grinding was a necessity. It was his way of life. If you took his way of life from him, he was already in prison.

Amanda practically begged him not to go back to Augusta before she finally fell asleep on his chest. Her pleading wasn't in vain, because she had persuaded him to stay a little while longer.

He looked down at her and couldn't help but smile. There wasn't a doubt in his mind that she was down for him. This was one of the few times in his life he wished that he could square up and live right, but he knew that was only a dream.

If Kruger wouldn't have called and told him that he had the new statement from Buck, he probably wouldn't be so anxious to get back to his city. In Savannah he felt out of place, especially since the demise of Big Wade. That incident had him questioning Firebug at times.

In his heart he wanted to believe that he could live the perfect life with the perfect woman and the perfect comrades, but he knew that life just wasn't perfect. So with that said he knew that he couldn't follow his heart.

It was never his intentions to have Kruger holding the fort down the way he was. Not that he couldn't trust him in that position, but because he knew it was an equal responsibility of them both. He hated feeling so helpless and out of place, that's why he'd already made up his mind. He was returning to what made him feel whole.

-TERESA-

Right now this nigga is on the phone with his cousin from Miami. When I gave him the phone I could tell that he didn't like the fact that I answered it. I really don't know what I was thinking about, but it really doesn't matter to me, I bought him that dam phone!

"Baby, who was that?" I asked after he hung the phone up and placed it on the coffee table.

"I thought we already talked about this shit you be pulling?" He stressed with a devilish expression.

Everytime he opened his mouth, it felt as he was trying to intimidate me or something, so to let him know I wasn't scared of him, I pressed on, "You still haven't answered my dam questioned."

"Why you tripping like that?" Now he's frustrated, "Now if you think that I'm going to Charlotte with your crazy ass acting like this, you definitely got it twisted!"

Now he hit a nerve, cause I knew that this was something he's been waiting to bring to the table, "I know you don't wanna go nowhere with me!" I stressed with aggression as I raised from the couch and headed towards the bedroom.

We were just watching a show together but I guess you can say that I just spoiled that. It's not like I wanted to spoil it or anything, but I feel that he really don't give a dam about me at times. Now what real woman would sit there with a man like everything is all good, knowing in her heart it ain't?

He must have stopped in the kitchen before he followed me to the bedroom, because he has a glass of ice in hand. Lord knows that he's gonna eventually drank himself to death before it's all over.

Something told me that I should've left well enough alone, but I had a few questions that I needed answers to, so hell, I asked, "Deamon, why you can't confide in me, I mean what am I really to you?"

Either that was the wrong question to start off with or he is really just tired of hearing my mouth. From the gruesome look he just gave me you would think that I just poured sugar in his gas tank or something.

"We done had these conversations over and over before, but I see that we didn't get any understanding out of it the first five time," he stated in a calm manner before pouring him a glass of cognac.

I watched him drank two full glasses before he turned to me and said, "I have a lot on my plate these days, so I apologize if I haven't been giving you enough attention. But you must understand that some things have to be tended to immediately," he paused for a moment before pouring another glass and adding, "maybe we just rushed into this relationship thing."

Now I'm the one dumbfounded. I was looking for him to say anything but what he just came out his mouth with, "You sound as if you've been thinking about this?"

"I have," he slurred out as I heard the cognac taking effect in his every word.

He stared at me for another second before saying, "You deserve more than what I have to offer right now, so maybe we need to chill for a minute."

I felt the tears coming so I buried my face with the pillow before I let my pride get in the way, "If that's what you wanna do."

"Listen baby-girl, if you don't wanna split for a few, then we don't have to. But you have to know that I have to feel secure around you, and these days I can't say that I'm feeling that way."

Now that made me pull that pillow from my face, "What you mean you don't feel secure around me?!"

When I looked in his eyes I could see that he was hurting just as much as I was, and that brought chills over my body. I never knew, until this moment, that he was so far out of my reach.

"We're living in to different worlds right now, and that's where our problems start," he added before drinking another glass.

"Why can't you just get an honest job, you don't have to be in the streets like you do, we can really make this work," I stated as the tears flowed freely down my cheeks.

He just smiled as he wiped the tears from my cheeks, "You already know that you're too beautiful to be crying," he whispered before he kissed me on my cheek.

I melted instantly. All I wanted was for us to be the perfect couple, have our baby and be the perfect family. People may think that I'm a fool for how I feel for him, but once you're in the mix, it's hard to bail out.

"Well, what about our baby?" I asked him.

"You already know the answer to that."

And he's right, I did. I knew if nothing else would, our baby would slow him down. I knew that he would go all out for his family, I guess that was another reason I tried to keep him so close to me. I couldn't help but start laughing because I realized that I'd turned into that foolish woman who never did any rational thinking when it came down to my emotions.

"You alright?" He asked me.

It took me a moment to gain my composure before I answered him, "I'm just tripping on how crazy all of this is."

He just smiled at the thought and I knew that it was still hope for us.

****

The clock on the DVD player read 9:37pm, and Weasel and Ericka was lounging on the couch watching Mario Puzo's, *'The Last Don'*, when his phone rang.

"What up Weasel?" He heard Jimmy ask.

"What's up with you playboy?" He replied.

"I need to get at you about that plug you say you have," Jimmy stated.

"Man, cease all that reckless talking on this horn, come through!" He retorted.

"I should be there in a minute, I'm right down the street."

Weasel just hung the phone up with a disgusted expression.

"Is he coming over?" Ericka asked as she glared up at him.

With his advice she made a change for the better. Her hair was cut in a sexy Halle Berry style that fit her oval face. She wore no extras, everything that was attached to her body, GOD had blessed her with.

"Yeah, he coming through," he reluctantly replied.

She raised from under him and headed towards the bedroom. She wore her teal colored braw and matching thongs, that gave him an instant hardening when he saw how her backside was jiggling. To him, she was his personal Luke dancer, and he let her know it every chance he got.

Right before she reached the bedroom door he started chanting, "I wanna rock, I wanna rock, I wanna rock, I wanna rock, I, I, I, I, I, I, do do brown, do do brown!"

She immediately started dancing at the door, making her backside bounce like the women in the Luke videos. From the way she was grinning, she was enjoying it just as much as he was.

"Baby, if we was in the club you could get all my money," he stated as she sashayed in the bedroom.

He could hear her giggling right before she stepped back in with a her black robe on.

"What you put that on for?" He asked openly disappointed.

"Don't you have company coming over?" She replied as she climbed over him, "I can't just let anybody see me like that, my man would kill me," she added with a sly grin.

"I see that you're pushing for wifey material," he stressed with a broad smile of his own.

"And you know it!" She retorted as she grabbed him through his shorts.

"Now why you starting shit when you know we ain't got time to finish?" He managed to whine out.

"Who said that we ain't got enough time?" She rebutted right before they heard the knock at the door.

"That says we don't," he replied as he lightly pushed her off him and raised up to answer the door.

After Jimmy walked in, Ericka spoke before she raised from the couch and headed towards the bedroom.

"So, what you looking to grab?" Weasel asked.

"At least four," he replied as he took a seat at the small breakfast table.

"You must be sitting on a hundred stacks?"

"If that's what it takes."

"Say no more," he replied as he grabbed his phone and walked in the bedroom.

After a few moments on the phone he walked back in front where Jimmy waited impatiently.

"My peoples said to meet him in *Bi-lo* parking-lot on Tobacco Road, in a half an hour."

"Well, let's ride and smoke one why we wait," Jimmy suggested.

Weasel walked back in the bedroom and put on his sneakers and a t-shirt before he kissed Ericka on the cheek and said, "I'll be back in like an hour."

Thirty minutes later they were pulling into the designated spot. To Jimmy's surprise, Kruger was waiting in his Coupe Deville, so he pulled next to him.

"Ya'll come and get in here with me, but make sure your back passenger door is unlocked," Kruger stressed.

Jimmy popped his trunk and grabbed a blue book bag before jumping in the passenger seat.

"Ya'll have all that cheese straight?" Kruger asked as he pulled off towards the neighborhood behind the grocery store.

"Let me double check the money back here," Weasel stressed from the backseat.

Kruger and Jimmy looked over at each other with puzzled expression before Jimmy passed Weasel the bag and said, "That should be a hundred right there."

Kruger just shook his head in disgust as Weasel never bothered to count the money, he just grabbed four grand off top and stuffed the money in his pockets.

Kruger continued to eye Weasel before he stressed, "I have somebody putting that in the car, so ya'll can just leave that bag, cause I left mine with ya'll."

When he pulled next to the Infiniti he reached under the seat and grabbed an ounce of granddaddy and handed it to Jimmy and said, "That's for shopping with a playa."

"Preciate that," Jimmy replied with a wide grin as he nervously eased out of the car.

"It's all there playboy," Weasel stated as he eased out behind Jimmy, "But, if you have a problem, just hit me up."

Kruger didn't verbally respond, but he did shake his head in disgust as Weasel slammed the door shut.

As Jimmy drove Weasel back to Ericka's he said, "I didn't know that he was doing it like that."

"I told you he was a hustler first," Weasel implied, "besides he has people in Florida, so I knew he wasn't gonna stay at the bottom too long."

"That's the business," Jimmy stressed.

Weasel just smiled as he gazed over at Jimmy and stated, "I know you might think that you just paid a little too much for them units, but I bet you feel better that you're coping from a real muthafucka. I'd pay the high-high all day for some security on my package. Fuck around and catch a sweet deal and we'd probably find ourselves in the same position we was in a few weeks ago.

-KRUGER-

Man, Ron just called and told me that Teresa over there spilling out her guts to Toya. I guess that's cool, cause that's her peoples and everybody needs somebody to talk to. But she has to understand, that if I don't get this money and my priorities in perspective, we won't have nothing to offer our child in the future.

I mean, what I look like struggling, just because. I watched my mama them go through that shit with us. Hell, that's when I decided that I was gonna find a way to bypass that arena. True enough, money ain't everything, but in order to live comfortable, a playa has to have something. It ain't like I'm trying to get all the paper, I just wanna be comfortable. I mean how long do we really supposed to struggle?

With all that said, these dudes Weasel and Jimmy has been on my mind lately. I mean Weasel really showed me that other side when he clipped his man for that little cheddar. I wanted to scream on him, but it wasn't my place. If I haven't learned nothing else these last few years, I learned to mind my own. Now, I just feel that I'm more aware of what he will and won't do.

It wasn't nothing for him to get something off top for the deal, but let that be known. Why would you try to skim it off the top? That's trifling, especially if you're skimming off your own people.

He had already hit me up with that crazy shit about Tom-Tom, and that wasn't kosher at all. It ain't no way I'm informing somebody about who bodied who. Calling your homie for advise is one thing, but informing him about some shit like that, is life threatening, for me and him. It's gonna be interesting to see how that there pan out.

As far as this money mission is concerned, I'm not interested in breaking these birds down right now, I just don't have the patience. I guess I don't possess that drive anymore to get out there and grind every brick out. Too much risk and too much time consuming. Yeah, it's definitely a bigger profit, but with the prices I'm presented with right now, I'd only be putting myself out there a little more than I have to, and I definitely don't need that extra heat.

Vito say that he trying to come see me real soon, him and Luther still trying to get me on their team. Don't get it twisted I think that's cool, but I'm in the mix of some other shit right now. Besides, they fucking with that dogg food, and I really don't have too much knowledge with that. Besides, I'm mentally drained from all the bullshit that goes on in my everyday life as it is, I don't need nothing extra right now.

All in all though, shit has to get better. Now, I'm suppose to go and look at this house off of Tobacco Road with Deidra tomorrow. I wanna do the same for Teresa, but I'll just probably end up getting her another car or some shit like that. I'm tired of her wanting to drive my Coupe or the truck anyway.

"Say bra," Lil Man has snuck up on me.

Naturally, I would be upset with somebody interrupting me and my time with the stars, but I'd break my back for baby bra, so he good.

"What's really good playboy?" I replied as I raised from the hood of the Coupe.

"You alright?" He asked with a concerned expression.

I had to crack a smile at this eleven year old future basketball hall of famer, "Yeah bra, I'm just out here clearing my mind," I replied, "what, mama sent you out here?"

STILL STUCK

"Man, it's 11:30, they sleep," he
responded as he climbed on the hood with me.

"So, what you doing up?" I had to ask.

"I guess you can say that I have a lot of
things on my mind too," he replied with a smirk.

(CHAPTER 4)

Jimmy sat in a folding chair with his arms folded on the steel table. He been in the grim looking interrogation room for over an hour, with Detective Mc'neil sitting across from him.

"So Mr.Kliene, when was the last time you saw Mr.Russell alive?" The detective questioned.

"A couple of days before he was arrested," he answered with a blank expression.

"And what were you two talking about?"

"It really was nothing," Jimmy responded with a light smile, "we was just talking about hitting the strip clubs in Columbia the next day."

"What strip club?" The detective challenged.

Jimmy just looked at him as if he'd been disrespected before he replied with, "All of them."

The detective just shook his head before asking, "Could you explain to me your relationship with Mr. Russell?"

"We were associates, nothing more, nothing less."

"You wouldn't call him a friend?"

"Detective, you and I both know that everybody that smiles in your face ain't a friend."

Detective Mc'neil rose from his seat with a disgruntled expression and walked out of the door that was labeled I-A and into the door that read I-B. The only difference in the two rooms were the occupants.

"Mr. Daniel Ford," he stated as he entered the room, "Or should I call you Weasel?"

"Call me what you like, just get this here over with," Weasel replied openly uncomfortable.

"If you haven't done anything wrong, then you have nothing to worry about," the detective assured him with a sly grin.

"The last time the police told me that, I ended up doing seven months in *Milledgeville's YDC* for some he say she say shit."

"First of all, I would like you to respect me just as I do you, so if I don't curse, you don't curse."

"I can go for that," he replied as he folded his hands together and placed them on the table, "now how can I assist you detective."

Detective Mc'neil just smiled before he implied, "I just wanted to know when was the last time you saw Mr. Russell alive?"

"A couple of days before he was arrested."

"What were you doing?"

"Just talking about this stripper from Dolls downtown."

"What was her name?"

"I don't know her real name, but her stage name was Venom, do you know her?" Weasel asserted with a sly grin.

"I can't say that I do," he replied with an irritated expression.

"You should check her out sometime, she's straight."

"Let's get something straight, Mr. Ford!" The detective stressed with aggression, "I ask the questions and you answer them!"

Weasel chuckled before asking, "Do you think that you can respect me as much as you want me to respect you?"

"Now, what makes you think that I don't have respect for you?" He cross-examined with a sinister grin.

Weasel raised from his seat before saying, "The last thing you wanna do is play with a grown man's intelligence!"

Detective Mc'neil stood up, "You first have to present yourself as a grown man to be considered as one."

Jimmy was in the parking lot waiting on Weasel. When Weasel finally reached the Q-45 a unmarked Taurus pulled up next to them. After the driver let down the tinted window he noticed that Honeycutt was sitting in the passenger seat, but he didn't know who the blond headed woman that was driving, but she did look familiar.

"I just stopped by to let ya'll know that we'll be in touch," Honeycutt stated with a sinister grin of his own.

"And we'll be waiting," Weasel replied before stepping in the Infiniti.

"What that muthafucka talking about?" Jimmy asked as he turned the sounds of *Outkast* down.

"The same thing them cats up stairs was talking about," Weasel assured him, "not a dam thing!"

After a few moments he looked over at Jimmy and asked, "Did everything go alright up there?"

"Yeah, but he ain't ask no helluva questions."

"Hell, the last person who really saw the nigga alive was the officer who escorted him out of jail that morning," he stated with a wide grin before adding, "so what could he have really asked you?"

STILL STUCK

****

Kruger pulled in front of 1122 in his Coupe Deville and hopped out. After Butler heard him step on the porch he walked up the hall from the back room.

"What's up Kruger?"

"What up Butler, where everybody at?" He replied as he took a seat in Hamburger's regular seat.

"They all just walked around to *Spur* to get some tater logs."

"So how has everything been going down here?"

"Everything been all good."

"Has Pimp been around?"

"He comes through every now and then, but he usually down there grinding with Kay-Kay."

Kruger rose from his seat before stressing, "I'm gonna walk down there and see what's-what."

After turning down a few smokers he finally noticed Vader sitting on the porch.

"Kruger!"

"What up Vader?" He replied as he climbed the few steps and sat next to him.

"Kruger, Kruger, Mr. 38 Ruger!" Vader responded as he saw Kruger walk up the steps, "Ain't nothing really popping around here, just been tripping off how those two in there argue like they've been married for years."

"They must be fucking or something?" Kruger found himself asking.

Vader looked over at him as if he'd done lost his mind before replying with, "Man, you know that she ain't gonna let you off the hook like that."

"Fool, what the hell you talking about?" He managed to stutter out.

"Man, you already know that these females can't hold water," Vader replied with a sly grin.

"So what is it she told you?"

"Just know, that I know, that you have business to tend to, and don't worry about me letting that sexy little thing in that Honda know anything."

Kruger grabbed him by the collar and stressed, "I know we ain't gotta worry about that!"

"You know that I ain't gonna disrespect like that!" He retorted as Kruger released him, "Dam, do I look that stupid?"

"Just as long as you know," Kruger stated as he raised up and headed towards the door.

"But you might need to check her on that shit she cooked up," Vader implied before he made it to the door.

"It was that bad?"

"Na'll, but it wasn't that good either."

"What about Pimp shit?"

"She helped him cook his."

"Why didn't you help them?"

"Man you know that one arm freak ain't gonna let me help him do nothing. He think that I'm gonna get something off the top, and you can't blame him, cause he right," he assured with a sinister grin.

Kruger just shook his head before walking in the house. The first person he noticed was Pimp fast asleep on the couch. He attempted to wake him up by slamming the door shut, but Pimp didn't budge. So he walked past him and into Kay-Kay's room.

He found her practically in the same position. She wore a pair a drawstring type shorts that was pulled tight between her legs so her camel-toe was fully exposed. Her tight t-shirt revealed the fact that her nipples were rock hard.

He climbed over her and placed his hand over her mouth, causing her to fight for breath. After her eyes were fully focused and she recognized that it was him over her, she calmed down.

He then put his finger over her lips and whispered, "You have to be quiet, Pimp is knocked out on the couch."

She grinned as she nodded her head and he started pulling her shorts off. After taking off her thongs he reached in his pocket and grabbed a piece of gum and fed it to her, "That's just in case you have that dragon."

He then rose from off her before practically demanding, "Do something with that shirt while I snatch off these clothes."

She took her shirt off in record time and was waiting for him to do the same. The moment he had it off, she grabbed him and pulled him on the bed.

"Dam, you ain't gonna let me take my shorts and shit off?"

"I got that," she stressed as she pulled his shorts and boxers to his thighs and bent over and practically slammed her mouth on his dick.

After feeling his body tense up, she looked up at him with a devious smile. She sucked on his dick until she felt that he couldn't get any harder, before she decided to straddle him.

After allowing him to marinate inside of her she whispered, "I missed this."

He remained silent as he noticed the beads of sweat forming up on her forehead.

"I knew you wanted this pussy," she stated as she started grinding on him.

He squeezed each of her ass cheeks and started to force her on him harder. Just when he was hitting deeper spots, she froze on top of him as she gave out a load moan.

"Kruger, I'm coming!" She stuttered out.

He didn't even give her time to regain her composure from her first orgasm as he crawled from under her and positioned her on her hands and knees. With no hesitation, he kicked his boxers and shorts off before entering her from behind.

He thrust in and out of her as if he was punishing her for all her foolish deeds. It wasn't but a few moments later when she started to meet his fierce penetrations with an impetus stride of her own. In her mind, if he was gonna punish her, she was going to take her punishment with pride.

After moments of her screaming from the top of her lungs and meeting his every stroke, he couldn't help but erupt.

He pulled out of her and shot his semen all over the bed. She spun around and quickly took him back in her mouth. After feeling that she had swallowed the rest of his juices and he was fully erect, she straddled him again.

The expression on her face excited him more than anything as she galloped on top of him. She bit her bottom lip as she dug her nails into his chest. He grabbed her hands and folded them into his as she continued to slam on top of him.

"AAAaahhhhhh," she continued to whine out.

Moments later she leaned over and lightly bit his chest as all of her juices exploded over his dick.

When she regained her composure she rose up from over him with a wide grin before saying, "Now, that's what's up!"

He lightly pushed her off of him with a sly grin before stressing, "You need to get a rag or something."

"I got that boo, I got that," she replied with a wide grin as she walked out of the room naked.

He was about to protest her walking out of the room like that, but he reminded himself not to get too carried away with her.

"Pimp is still asleep on the couch," she stated as she stepped back in with a few rags.

"After all that noise you were making, I thought that you had woke up the neighborhood," he replied as she started to clean him off.

The moment she finished him he started to put his clothes back on, and she walked back in the bathroom. When he stepped in the living room he slapped Pimp across the head and yelled, "There go them folks playboy, we gotta hit the back!"

Pimp jumped up with eyes wide open as he headed towards the back door.

Kruger burst out laughing and said, "At least you ain't slipping that bad."

"Nigga, you know better than to be playing like that!" He retorted as he sat back on the couch breathing hard and scratching his head.

"What up though, is you getting your money right?"

"Yeah my nigga," he stated with a wide grin, "I mean, I'm making my share."

"That's what's up, but if ya'll need to ree-up, ya'll need to let it be known," he stated before pausing and adding, "and I heard about that bullshit ya'll cooked up, ya'll know that you can't do nothing but lose like that."

"I told that silly ass bitch that shit, but she know too dam much as it is, so she can't be told nothing!"

"I'll holler at her on that, you just get right," Kruger stated before raising from the couch and walking towards the door, "I'll be back in a little while to see if ya'll ready to do something, I gotta make a move right now though."

As he walked out the door Vader stressed, "Dam Kruger, you had that girl hollering like a muthafucka!"

"Man, shut the fuck up?!" He retorted.

"Na'll nigga, you shut the fuck up!" He rebutted, "You owe me cause some little cutie in a green Acura came through looking for you about twenty minutes ago."

"Dam, what she riding through here for?" He asked more to himself than anything.

"She said she tried to call you but you didn't answer the phone," Vader implied.

Kruger grabbed his phone from his pocket and he had two missed calls from Teresa, so he called her back.

-TERESA-

Now am I so wrong for trying to spend some time with my man? Dam, I hate him sometimes. How he gonna call me with that crazy ass attitude because I rode down his precious ass Summer Street! Man fuck Summer Street!

I mean he ain't never just say that it was forbidden for me to travel that route. I'm already aware that it's dangerous down there, but he didn't have to go off on me like that.

"Teresa, Toya is on the phone for you," I hear Tamika say from the kitchen.

"Yeah Toya," I dragged out after I picked up the phone from off the night stand.

"And hey to you too," she sarcastically replied.

Lord knows that I ain't in the mood to be hearing her ongoing nagging.

"Look Toya, I already have enough bullshit to put up with today."

"Dam, how you let that young nigga get you worked up like that!" She blasted, "Every since he brought you that car he's been my baby this, my baby that."

I know that she's been envious of the Vigor every since I pulled up at her job in it, but she be going overboard and turning that envy to pure hatred. She's really hot at the fact that I'm doing a little better than her on the financial tip.

"Na'll, it ain't Deamon this time, it's the crazy people at that prison," I found myself saying.

It ain't no way that I'm gonna let her feel that she can pick me like that, not when I know all she wanna do is hate on the side.

"Yeah whatever," she stressed before implying, "but sis, I need you to do me a favor."

The last time she called me sis in that tone, I was lying to her mama about her and Eddie, so I knew this was some outrageous shit.

"What is it?"

"Just promise me you'll do it?"

"Na'll, you have to tell me what it is first."

"I need you to ride back to Savannah with me this weekend."

"We can do that," I stated a little enthused.

Now heading back home wasn't such a bad idea, but something told me that it was more to it.

"But what are you talking about doing?" I just had to ask.

"Well," she's dragging this shit out, "David and Eddie are in the county jail for some old warrants, I thought we could go and see them."

"Toya, I thought you were through with that?!"

"I am Tee," she whined out, "The only reason that I wanna see Eddie is because I never wrote and told him about Ron. So I wanna at least step up and tell him to his face."

"Well, I ain't going, because I don't wanna see David!"

"You know that I need you on this one Tee," she's whining again, "I feel more comfortable knowing that you'll be there to have my back."

"What does Ron say about it?"

"He doesn't know," she had the nerve to say.

Now either Eddie use to eat the hell out of her pussy, or she really needs a mental evaluation.

"Toya," I stated in the calmest manner I could conjure up, "You are losing your mind."

"Tamika, ain't around you is she?"

"Na'll, she's deep into that geometry book, so she ain't thinking about neither one of us right now."

"Listen Tee, this is just something that I have to do. Now, I'm asking you as a friend to come with me."

Now that did it. How am I suppose to tell her no after a remark like that.

"What makes you think that they even want to see us?" I asked trying to find the perfect escape route out of this drama."

"Because Eddie called my mama and told her that he wanted to see me," she replied before pausing and adding, "To be honest with you, I think that they're both back to snitch on somebody and get lesser time."

"I can't believe that they're still cool after what Eddie did to him."

"Now that's none of our business," she rebutted just like I knew she would, "but I still need you on this one."

I hated the fact that she was putting me in this position, but the fact still remained that David was a demon I had to face, so I found myself saying, "I gotcha girl."

"Well, we leaving tomorrow, and since you're the one with the fly whip, you're driving," she managed to giggle out.

"Whatever," I stated not as enthused as I was before.

"Thank-you Tee," I heard her say with a sigh of relief before she hung up.

I have to find where it says to help a friend, you must deceive your lover, because I know that's all I'm doing to Deamon.

✳✳✳✳✳✳✳✳✳✳✳✳✳✳✳

Gunslanga sat in the passenger seat of Amanda's Altima as she drove him down Summer

Street. She couldn't help but notice the wide grin on his face after seeing Kruger and the fellas on the porch.

She'd did all the protesting she could do, but he'd already made up his mind about. The more she protested, the quicker he was packing, so she eventually left well enough alone.

She pulled next to Kruger's Caddy and watched her man rolled down the window.

"Brrraaaa!" he called out.

All the fellas turned to see who it was, but before anyone could really respond Kruger was already making his way to the car.

Without saying a word Kruger jumped in the back-seat and demanded her to pull off.

"Nigga, is you done lost your mind!" Kruger blasted.

She couldn't help but smile at his outburst before revealing, "I tried to tell him."

Gunslanga just looked over at the both of them and shook his head before stressing, "I'm here now, so hate it or love it."

"Playboy, I just don't wanna see you fucked up. Why you ain't call and let me know that you was coming?" Kruger stressed in a concerned manner.

"Cause I knew that you were gonna try to talk me out of coming!" He replied as he turned all the way around in his seat to face Kruger, "But my nigga, you know that this hustle shit is in my blood, and besides who's gonna hold shit down while you're in Charlotte."

"I can feel you on that," Kruger replied but openly not comfortable with the decision his comrade had made ,"but you have to understand that you're no good to a nigga locked up."

Gunslanga just turned back around in his seat and looked out of the passenger window before asking, "So what would you have had for me to do playboy, rot in that apartment."

Kruger and Amanda looked at each other through the rear-view mirror with mutual concerned on their faces.

"Say Amanda, get your phone and call Deidra for me," Kruger stressed before taking his eye off of her and adding, "we just coped this crib out there in the county and ya'll welcome to stay until all this shit clear up."

"Oh yeah, nigga," he stated as he turned back around to face his comrade, "ya'll done coped a crib?"

Kruger just smiled after seeing how hype his comrade got about it, "Yeah, four bedrooms, two baths, a little something-something."

"Now see what the fuck I'm talking about!" He stressed as he looked over at Amanda, "I'm slipping like a muthafucka!"

Kruger just shrugged his shoulders with a wider grin as they rode towards Tobacco Road.

✱✱✱✱✱✱✱✱✱✱✱✱✱✱

"So what's the word Weasel?" Baby Gotti was asking as he walked out of his house.

"Anything you need B.G.," Weasel replied as he sat on the hood of his convertible.

Baby Gotti was a 17 year old hustler with his own everything. Him and his partner, Lil Dusty, robbed and killed a Cuban for a kilo of cocaine when they were 14, and neither of the two apparently ever looked back, at least that was the word on the street.

"Well, the last thing you brought through was on point, so if you're working with the same shit, I wanna grab two," Baby Gotti pointed out before lighting the blunt he had in his hand.

"Dam homie, I might have to let you holler at one of my peoples, cause if I throw you a number, you might feel I'm being disrespectful."

"It don't matter to me where it comes from, just as long as your peoples ain't the police."

Weasel just smirked at the comment before replying with, "You should know better than that."

"So what's the hold up?"

"Let me holler at my peoples first and then I'll get back at you," Weasel responded as he walked towards his convertible.

"What, you need a phone or something," Baby Gotti implied as he passed him the blunt before he added, "I needed them things like yesterday."

Weasel couldn't help but smile at the way Baby Gotti handled himself. If it wasn't for his baby face you would have thought the youngster was close to thirty. Just when Weasel pulled his phone out of his pocket, a young girl came to the door and called Baby Gotti.

"What's up?" He replied.

"Lil Dusty on the phone," she yelled back.

"Bring me the phone," he stressed as Weasel grabbed his the phone.

Weasel was talking to Jimmy while Baby Gotti was engaged in a conversation with Lil Dusty.

"I need to know what the lowest you would let one of them cakes go for?" Weasel asked Jimmy.

"For you?"

"Of course, for me!" Weasel replied with aggression.

"Twenty-seven."

"Dam playboy, you must have extra nuts on that red velvet!" Wease l stressed.

"Something like that, but it's beyond red, it's almost burgundy and it's moist as hell."

"Man, you're lucky I need it right this minute," Weasel spat out.

"Na'll nigga, you're lucky that I got it right this minute."

Weasel just chuckled before stating, "I'll hit you up and let you know where we gonna meet in a few."

"Do that."

"Be safe playboy," Weasel stressed before hanging the phone up.

"So what's the word?" Baby Gotti asked after he finally was off his phone.

"He screaming that he down to his last, so he needs like twenty-nine a piece for his," Weasel replied as a cat pulled up behind him in a black *SS* Monte Carlo.

"I thought you said you was gonna let me hollar at him?" Baby Gotti questioned.

Weasel heard him but he was more focused on the guy who had just jumped out of the *SS*. He watched as the guy stepped around his car and walk right up to Baby Gotti.

"What up B.G.?" He greeted as they gave each other dap.

"Nothing to funny Rock," Baby Gotti replied.

"I need to hollar at you," Weasel heard the cat say.

"It'll be a minute playboy, I'm waiting now," Baby Gotti responded as he grabbed the blunt from Weasel.

"Well, I'll get back at you a little later," the cat stated as he headed back to his car.

"You wanna sell that *SS*?" Weasel asked as he stepped out of the car.

"It looks like you're already straight playboy," the guy who went by the name Rock replied as he stopped and appraised Weasel's convertible.

"She's alright," Weasel replied with a sly grin, "but I need something I can punch when I wanna, and she sounded pretty good when you pulled up."

"What you talking about spending?" Rock inquired.

"I can't put no price on your shit," Weasel replied.

"If you really want her, I'll let her go for thirty-five hundred."

Weasel walked over and appraised the inside. After he saw that everything was pretty much intact he dug in his pocket and pulled out a huge knot of money.

"You got the papers on you?" He asked as he peeled the thirty-five hundred off the knot.

"Na'll, that at my lil shorty house she stay like two streets over. I'll bring them right back," he happily responded before jumping in the car.

Baby Gotti watched Rock ride off before looking over at Weasel and saying, "The nigga would be back to buying two ounces in a week."

"Why you say that?" Weasel questioned.

"He a powder head," Baby Gotti replied with a look of disgust.

"For each his own," Weasel spat out.

"Thank GOD for that!" Baby Gotti proclaimed before asking, "So how long it's gonna take for you to get that to me? As you can see, I'm already missing money."

-KRUGER-

Here I am sitting in the parking-lot of an apartment building, that I pay rent at, because I know that as soon as I step foot through the door, this girl gonna have something negative to say. A man is should not feel this uncomfortable about walking into his own crib. When shit get like that, you know it's far past the time to dip. The sad part about it, it's all my fault.

All of this extra drama accumulated because I didn't man up and let Teresa know what my intentions was when I hit the street. I don't know if she would've went for it or not, but at least that would've been on her and not me. Now, I find myself not being able to face the monster that I've obviously help create. Our relationship was built off fairytales, that's why I feel I just can't leave her by the waste side. I mean you got that and the fact that she's carrying my seed.

I want to let her know that I have another baby on the way from Deidra, but I gotta find the right way to do it. I mean, I just can't walk in there and say some shit like that, at least not right now, cause she really don't deserve that. It ain't her fault she is what she is. I knew what I was dealing with before I let it go this far. It's crazy cause I felt that I had everything under control, and now it's all about to blow up in my face. Besides, the dilemma with her and Deidra, I still have to keep my eye on Slanga's ass.

This cat just insist on getting his grind on, and who am I to stand in the way of that. After he went on the run, we agreed that we were 50/50 partners, so half of everything is his. He say that he don't feel right about me pulling the load like I've been doing, but under the circumstances, I had no choice.

Without a doubt, I respect his mind, but with all that said, I'm still not too cool with his decision. If you ask me, he's pushing it a little. But, all in all, he made it clear that my opinion on that is irrelevant.

We have like five or six of them things left, and I already know what he gonna do with them. He a grinder, so I can look for him to make no less than 40 off each one, he has patients on that aspect.

He stressed the fact that he didn't like Pimp being down there in his spot, which I understood. He say that was the only thing he had a problem with. So Pimp should be far away from Slanga trap by now.

153

Me and Deidra rented out this trailer off of Morgan Road to put the dope, so that's where Slanga is right now. He might be there for a minute, he say he gonna cook up at least two bricks. I helped him with a half, but I ain't about to be fucking with that shit all night.

Him and Amanda staying in the guest room at the crib. Deidra and my mama picked out some nice furniture for the crib so it's laid. Now all I have to worry about is my mama running her mouth to Teresa.

"Let me get my ass out of this car and face this demon," is all I was able to spit out before I eased out and up stairs.

When I stepped through the front door Tamika was at the table with her geometry book in front of her.

"Girl, it's almost ten o'clock and you still doing homework," I stressed as I passed her and went to the kitchen to get a cup of ice.

"Na'll, I'm studying for this test I have tomorrow," she replied with a frustrated expression.

"I wish I could help you but you know that I ain't on that level," I revealed before I asked, "where Teresa at?"

"She back there in the shower."

"You need anything while in the kitchen?"

"No, I'm alright," she replied before he walked out and headed down the hall towards the bedroom.

After I downed two glasses of *Hennessy* and poured me a third cup I walked to the bathroom. I could hear the sounds of Exscape's, '*Understanding*', humming through the door with Teresa singing along. When I opened the door the steam hit me dead in my face.

I walked to the shower curtain and opened it before saying, "I don't know why you in here with all this noise."

"Deamon!" She yelled as if I'd done something wrong, "You can't be sneaking up on people like that."

"You look like you were expecting someone else," I stressed before I slapped her on that fat ass.

"Stop fool!" she screamed out, "You know I'm wet!"

"Can I get in?" I asked with that look that told her I wanted to eat her alive.

She, in return, gave me that seductive expression and nodded her head. The way she was biting her bottom lip had me zoned out. This woman and these facial expressions really be having me in her twilight zone. Her eyes alone are a helluva distraction.

I downed that last glass of cognac before stripping and jumping in with her. After standing under the water for a moment, she turned me around and I gave her one of those kisses that said, I'm about to freak the hell out of you.

After our lips separated she asked, "What was that for?"

"You think of a reason," I replied as I grabbed the rag and the bar of *Black Soap.*

She blushed before implying, "Let me get that for you."

After lathering the soap in the rag she started bathing me.

"You know me and Toya are suppose to go to Savannah tomorrow," I heard her say as she washed my back.

"Do you need some money?"

"I don't need no money," she whined out, "I just wanted you to know so you wouldn't think I was running off or something."

"So, when ya'll suppose to be coming back?"

"Sunday night."

"Just make sure you call me if you need something."

"I will," she stated as I turned to face her.

"I wasn't finished washing your back," she stressed.

"We got all night for that," I stressed before I threw my tongue in her mouth with a little more passion then I had the first time.

✴✴✴✴✴✴✴✴✴✴✴✴✴✴

The digital clock on the night stand read 3:26am and Jimmy sat at the small table smoking a blunt while Surina was fast asleep in bed. As he sat there thinking about the nightmare he'd just had, he knew that he couldn't just lay

157

back down and deal with it, especially with Surina in the room.

He had been having the same dream every other night or so. He was being chased by Tom-Tom and a bunch of other zombie looking goons, who too, had holes in their heads. The crazy thing about the dream was the fact that every time he had it, Tom-Tom and his goons seemed to be getting closer and closer in the chase. The last time he had even got shot in the leg.

When he finally stumbled to the ground Tom-Tom walks up to him and shows him the two holes in his head and says, "Jim-bo, how could you do me like that, I took you in, I put some cash in your pockets, made you a man again!"

Somehow Jimmy managed to kick him away from him, struggle to his feet and hop to a nearby car. But when he gets in the car and tries to crank it, it won't start. So he jumps out and starts to hop away. He ends up running down this alley and when he finally built up the nerve to look back and see where Tom-Tom and the goons were, he sees that it's twice as many of them as it was before, with Tom-Tom leading the pack.

The next thing he knew Tom-Tom leaped from like twenty yards behind him and jumped on his back with this devilish laugh. Tom-

Tom slammed his head on the pavement as hard as he could causing Jimmy to lose focus. When he finally was able to open his eyes he realized that he was in the middle of the mob. They all just was looking down on him for a moment before Tom-Tom motioned for them to attack. That's when they all started to kick and stomp him. As they continued to stomp him he awaken.

When the dream first started Jimmy would've been the first to admit that he was really shaken up by it. But now Tom-Tom was coming way too often so they really didn't get the best of him anymore. The only reason he didn't want to lay back down that instant was Surina was laying right next to him. He didn't want to wake up in cold sweats with her questioning him about what was wrong.

With Tom-Tom in the back of his mind he really started to focus on making money on safer terms. Since Tom-Tom was gone, Jimmy had managed to accumulate most of his clientele. He was very picky about who he even conversed with about business. The way he looked at it, one of Tom-Tom's people were the reason the Feds had raided his crib in the first place.

Another thing that had him tripping was the fact that Weasel tried to play him for slow on the little transaction with Kruger. He wasn't concerned about him getting a few stacks behind the move, what concerned him was the way he got it. That move had him thinking about what Surina had once told him, "Why you think Deamon them don't fuck with him like that too funny, cause he's shady as hell and can't be trusted!"

He brushed that thought away from his mind and concentrated on his next task. He knew that he couldn't allow Weasel to be in the middle of his transaction, so his main focus was to get at Kruger. The way he looked at it, if it was left up to Weasel he'd forever pay the high-high.

-TERESA-

"Girl, I can't believe you got me going through this," I was stressing to Toya as we walked through the entrance of the Chatham County Jail.

"Teresa, you know I couldn't do this without you," she replied with a worrisome look, "but if I don't do it, I will never forgive myself."

I made up my mind right then that I wasn't gonna say anything else to her. I felt stupid for being there as we walked up to the reception desk.

"Hey Toya and Teresa," the big man looking lady greeted us.

I had to double take on her ass before I recognized who she was.

"Bridgette?" Toya asked in a questionable manner.

Just another irritation that I wasn't too moved to see. This is the same butch looking bitch who use to try and beat me up in middle school, and now it's her job to check us in and all that other bullshit before I have to see another muthafucka that I ain't too crazy about seeing. I was so ready to get the hell out of the lobby area and get this visit over with.

After watching and listening to Toya have small talk with the butch, we was placed in this room with like five cubicles. So me and Toya sat next to each other right in the middle, since nobody else was there.

In front of us was this three inch glass window with small holes in the frame, so I knew that we all would be yelling so the others could hear what we was saying. Me and Toya was laughing about something when David walked up to my cubicle.

"What's so funny?" He asked with that sexy, dimpled up smile.

Now I don't ever think I said how fine this cat is, but he is holding his down like a eighteen wheeler. He reminds you of this street but pretty boy type of cat. If I can recall, the first thing I remember that attracted me to him was those sexy ass dimples.

I really hate to admit it, but as soon as I saw those dimples, I melted and my pussy started throbbing. I was glad that Toya was there, she actually help me keep my mind off that crazy shit.

"Hey David, it looks like you've been hitting that iron," Toya stated as she leaned over in my cubicle.

And she wasn't lying either, Dam!

"What up Toya?" He replied without taking a second to even look at her.

I looked in his eyes and I could tell that he was holding back from blasting on her. The moment I saw this, I knew that he was aware of how she was so down with setting him up. I use to ask myself was he that blind, but seeing how he reacted, I knew he wasn't. But with all that said, I still couldn't understand why was he here with Eddie.

"Where Eddie at?" She asked him, after realizing that he had no conversation for her.

"I'm right here," I heard the fucker say.

I couldn't resist looking over in her cubicle, after seeing the bastard I couldn't resist saying, "Na'll Toya, I think Ron looks ten times better."

She was dumbfounded, and I don't think I could began to explain the expression on his face.

"So how you been?" David asked after I looked over at him.

"I'm alright, but I'm pregnant," I found myself spitting out before I realized what I had just said.

I wanted to tell him that off top. It was no need for me to feed him no bullshit, but I'm sitting here wondering why I got my head down and feeling so bad about it.

"I don't think that's something to be ashamed about," I heard him say before he asked, "does he know yet?"

"Yeah, he knows," I replied with my head still down.

"What did he say?"

"He's supportive, in his own way."

"Your hair looks nice."

"Thank-you," is all I found myself saying, because I didn't do anything but get a perm.

"Now, since you've got your complement, do you think that I can see a little more than that?" His sarcastic ass asked.

"Oh we got jokes?" I questioned as I raised my head with a smile.

"Somebody has to break the ice," he replied with that sexy ass smile.

"I guess you're right," I replied as I started fidgeting with my hands.

"You know that there's a lot shit I wanna say to you, and there's a lot of things I wanna ask you too," he stated as I saw my dimples disappear, "but I pretty much already

164

know how you're gonna respond, and the type of answers that you'll likely come up with."

"So?"

"So, I'm not gonna waste this time with the irrelevant."

"So what are we gonna talk about?"

"I would like to talk about you and your plans for the future," he replied as those cute dimples came back.

Right then, at that moment, I wanted to put my tongue right there in the mist of that right dimple, just like I use to.

"For a minute I thought you was gonna say us," I found myself saying.

My dimples disappeared again before he stressed, "I told you that I refuse to talk about the irrelevant."

"We are not the irrelevant!" I snapped back, "And talk regular, you got me feeling like I'm back in school or some shit."

"Teresa, there is no more us, you've destroyed any future that we could ever had."

"Me?!" I retorted, "I ain't the one who got locked-up!"

"No, but you're the one who turned her back on the whole situation when I needed her the most," he stated with a look as if he was trying to see through me.

"What did you expect me to do?" I sternly asked before I put my head back down.

"You might as well lift your head back up, cause we can't get nowhere like that," he's aggravated now, "and for future references, that's a sign of weakness."

I found myself looking back into those hazel eyes of his and asking, "What do you want from me David?"

"There is nothing you can give me," he replied with a gruesome expression, "I've had everything you've had to offer, and I really don't want anything else to do with you."

Now you talk about a head buster, that shit there threw me for a loop, "Well, why the hell are you sitting in front of me?"

"To try and prevent you for making the same mistake twice."

"What the hell you mean, the same mistake twice?"

"That cat Deamon," I heard him say and instantly felt stupid as hell for being there.

"What about him?"

"He a real cat and I wish I would've meet him when I was out there," he stated before pausing and adding, "What he did for me is unthinkable. Sometimes I sit off in that cell and ask myself would I do the same for a nigga if the shoe was on the other foot."

"And?" I asked with a cold stare.

"And, I can't say that I would."

"How did ya'll start kicking it anyway?" I questioned.

"That's irrelevant. The point is, you have something good going with buddy, but you're so blind that you don't see it."

"How do you know what I see?" I asked with a smirk.

"Because you had something similar going on with me and soon as the heat came, you dipped."

"Look David," I had to interrupt him, cause I grew tired of him trying to low-grad me, "I never meant to hurt you. I never meant for any of this to happen."

"That was the same thing I was striving to tell you when I got locked-up."

He was obviously more prepared for the conversation than I was.

"I lost everything when you got locked-up," I pointed out, "my car and my job at the dentist office."

"You talking about the job I used my resources for you to get, and that car that I bought?" He sarcastically questioned, "See, you sitting here talking about that little shit that you lost, the same shit that you wouldn't even have if it wasn't for me. Now let's talk about the shit I lost."

If I didn't know that I'd hurt him before, he's definitely making me feel it right now.

"I lost my freedom, my friend, my companion and most importantly, my trust in you," he stressed as tears streamed down his face, "I hear you screaming about you this and you that, but let's take some time out to think about someone other than Teresa.

Now how many times did you go and check to see how my mama was doing?" He continued, "Now keep in mind, this is the same woman that you use to call mama too. Now, how do you think that makes her feel? Maybe you never saw that it wasn't all about me, if I was the only one hurt from your actions, I probably wouldn't be so bitter about it."

"David, I apologize, I wasn't thinking," I found myself crying out, "I just wanted out of that situation!"

I didn't come here to shed a tear about anything, but when you fucked up, you've fucked up.

"The feeling is mutual, cause I couldn't have been thinking," I could swear that his eyes had turned from hazel to a fire red, "I was just fooling myself by thinking that you of all people would be there for me. If you want to know the truth, I don't even blame you, I blame myself. Your boyfriend said some real shit in a letter that he wrote me. He said some shit like, some say that we are responsible for those we love, while others know that we are responsible for those who love us."

Have you ever felt stupid, dishonest and just plain out dead wrong all at the same time? If you have, then you are definitely feeling me right this instant.

"Why are you telling me this?" I asked as I tried to wipe my tears away.

"So, that maybe you'll grow to understand that you only get out what you put in. If you can't show love, don't look for it."

"I have never cheated on you David!" I retorted as I sat erect in my seat.

"And that maybe so, but being loyal goes way deeper than your sexual desires and decisions. The word you're looking for is faithful. Being faithful is just one of the many traits that goes under the word loyalty.

Being loyal to someone is being that person the other can depend on," he continued, "someone's who's there through the storm, not just there when it's clear outside."

What is this, Morals 101?

"Nigga, you ain't never told me shit! Now tell me, how could I be so prepared for something that I have no knowledge of?" I rebutted.

"And for that, I may be at fault. But, I have codes that I live by, just as your boy does. And if I know him like I think I do, he doesn't discuss nothing with you either. But there is gonna come a time when he's gonna need you, and if you're not there for him, he'll move on to the next thing with a blink of an eye."

"Now, why would you say some shit like that?!"

"Because he's already on point when it comes down to you. The little nigga is actually smarter than I was," he confessed with a sly grin.

The rest of the visit was bullshit so I was happy when we reached the car. Toya held her composure the entire time, but as soon as we were in the car she burst out crying.

"Are you alright?" I held her and asked.

"I still love him Tee," she whined out.

"But what about Ron?"

"I love him too, but that doesn't mean I don't love Eddie."

I could really understand where she was coming from, cause I sort of felt the same way.

"But girl you know you have to let Eddie go, Ron is your future now," I drilled in her head.

She nodded her head in agreement and I knew that she was going to be alright.

"Girl, you don't need to be crying," I said to her after letting her go, "tears don't go to well with your mascara."

She just lightly giggled before finally replying with, "Dam you."

(CHAPTER 5)

-KRUGER-

Teresa finally got me trapped up here in Charlotte feeling uncomfortable. This has officially been the worst week I've had since I've been free.

Just being around Teresa and her prissy ass cousins, really irks me. For some strange reason she feels that she has to shine in front of them. They the type of females that drive Jaguars, but live in those way too small space, two bedroom apartments. Nine times out of ten they're up to their neck in debt for one thing or the other.

I normally wouldn't even stress the way they act, because it's really none of my business, people are going to be who they are despite how I feel. But listening to Teresa scream about her cousin Nicole, which by the way, happens to be one of the finest females I've ever laid my eyes on, but this broad is dingy as hell.

STILL STUCK

Nicole is suppose to be one of the top criminal attorneys in the state, but her crazy ass laugh irks the hell out of me. It's like they all trying too hard to be friends.

Bambi is her first cousin who's cute in her own way, but everytime Teresa turns her head she gives me her look of seduction, where she slightly bites on her bottom lip. I called myself telling ole silly ass Teresa that her cousin a freak and how she be licking her lips at me, and she had the nerve to ask me what I did to make her feel that it was alright. I had to take a break from them for a minute, but I can honestly see why she acts the way she acts.

Here I am riding through Charlotte, blowing on a blunt, seeking for some peace. I just past by *Applebee's* on Independence. I was gonna walk in the *Gentlemen's Club*, but those half naked broads really don't bring me peace.

Sometimes I just sit and wonder why I allow myself to stay in the mist of this crazy shit. I mean, dealing with Deidra, Teresa and the streets seems to be too overwhelming at times. It's so much I have to balance out, but with Honeycutt and his goons always coming through to tilt the scale, I'm never really able to do just that.

Vito called me last night and said that he'll be in Augusta next week. Now with me knowing cuz, it ain't just to say what up, so that's something else that I have to be prepared for. Old man Luther probably sent him to try and recruit me again, but I won't know nothing until he gets here.

I talked to Black earlier too. That cat screaming that them folks been riding real hard looking for Slanga again, so I know it won't be long for they busting down that fool's door. He got this cat name Fredel in there grinding with him.

Fredel's a cool cat, me and him did some time together. He suppose to be Kay-Kay's cousin, but I'm still curious on how he's gonna handle everything.

I might need to take my ass back where this crazy ass broad at. She done hit me up twice already. Lord knows that I'm not in the mood to be hearing all that crazy talk. I'm trying to let her spend these last few hours with her family, cause it's a most I be back in Augusta tomorrow.

★★★★★★★★★★★★★★★

"Look folk," Baby Gotti was saying to his comrade Lil Dusty, "this nigga Weasel cool, but he ain't reliable enough."

They sat on the couch in Baby Gotti's living room while their girlfriends were in the kitchen cooking dinner.

"So what you suggest?" Lil Dusty asked.

When you looked at these two sitting there, they reminded you of the two cats DMX had under him in the movie *Belly*.

"I say we holler at your cousin Fredel, since he down there fucking with that nigga Slanga," Baby Gotti pointed out.

"I ain't think about that," Lil Dusty replied with a sly grin.

"I just feel that's a better move than just sitting here waiting on that cat Weasel. We can't win like this!" He replied with a look of disgust.

"I'll get at cuz right now," he stressed as he grabbed his phone off the coffee table.

Just when he dialed Fredel's number, someone rang the doorbell.

"Who is it?" Baby Gotti asked as he walked towards the door.

"This Rock," the voice replied from the other side.

"What up playboy, what you need?" He asked as he opened the door.

"I need a big eighth," he replied as he stepped in.

"Dam nigga you still copping four and halves?" Baby Gotti questioned with a disturbed expression, "You caught a lick on that car you sold the other day, so why sell yourself short?"

"Man, I had a lot of shit to deal with, so now I'm able to grind for me," Rock replied.

Baby Gotti examined him closer and noticed the powder residue at the tip of his nose and decided to let it go, Rock wasn't his concern.

If he hadn't learned nothing else early on, he'd learned to mind his own. You can't turn a beggar to a hustler or a whore into a house-wife. All of that required too much time, and that was just something they felt they didn't have at the moment, not with the mission they were on.

"True, I respect that," was all Baby Gotti responded with as he walked out the back door.

A few moments later Rock was walking out of the house a satisfied customer and Lil Dusty was off the phone with his cousin.

"Man do you think that nigga Rock is ever gonna make it past a four and a baby?" Baby Gotti asked his comrade.

"Hell na'll!" Lil Dusty retorted, "He trick too much with them broads and he keeps shoveling that shit up his nose."

"I was thinking the same thing."

"Man fuck Rock, let me put you on point on what cuz-o screaming," he excitedly stressed.

"What up?"

"He say that he gonna hollar at Slanga and see what he talking about. H also say he might can get us a better number too."

Baby Gotti smiled at the thought of having a reliable connect. With them being so young, a lot of heavy rollers were reluctant to do business with them. Word around town was, they were too young, and young cats draw too much heat. But Baby Gotti knew if they got tied in with Slanga, they never had to worry about where their next pack was coming from.

- KRUGER-

"Say Kruger," I hear Slanga calling my name.

I wasn't gonna answer him, but Deidra pushed me on my back, so I had to get up.

"What up bra?"

"I need to hollar at you before I head down the way," he replied.

I raised my head from the pillow and looked over past Deidra to the clock on the nightstand and couldn't believe that it read 9:03am.

"Man give me a minute," I stated in a frustrated manner as I rolled out of bed.

When I looked over at Deidra she just gave me a silly look before covering her head with her pillow. She had one of those paisley head wraps on that had her looking too sexy. Lord knows I could really get use to waking up with her.

STILL STUCK

When I walked out of our bedroom and into the living room, I found Slanga's silly ass pacing the living floor with a glass of orange juice in hand.

"Now what's so important that you had to wake me and ole girl up at nine in the morning?" I asked as I flopped on the couch.

"I just wanted you to know that I put some of that info to use the other night," is what I heard this fool say.

"Say what?!" I asked as I sat up, "On who?"

"I got them cats Martin, Sanchez and Olgetree."

"I mean what happened, how did you hit them with it?"

"I told them that I had five grand a piece to let me know about any bust in the hood, at least a few hours before it's going down."

"And all three of them were cool with it?"

"Yeah," he answered with a smile, "all I did was call Sanchez and he hollered at the other two. At first he was like na'll, but then I reminded him about where his two daughters go to school at and what their teacher's name was." He added with a devilish grin.

You gotta love this cat.

"So it's gonna cost us fifteen grand a month for three agents?"

"Pretty much," he replied with a smirk.

"What about the detectives who been looking for you on that other shit?"

"They was like they couldn't do nothing about that cause that's another division, but from what they hear about the case, they really don't have nothing on a playa."

"That ain't nothing we don't already know," I replied as I walked towards the kitchen.

"True, but it felt good hearing it from one of them," I heard him say as I grabbed the orange juice out of the fridge and poured myself a glass.

I felt where he was coming from. I don't think nobody was a 100% sure that he was gonna come off clean.

"I'm about to let Amanda meet Martin's wife with this money," he stressed as I walked back in the living room.

"How much you need from me?" I asked before drinking all the juice in one gulp.

I don't know why I always do that. I could've did that in the kitchen and put the glass in the sink. Now seven times out of ten, I'm gonna leave the glass on the coffee table and have to hear Deidra screaming about it later.

"I got this one playboy, you just catch next month's bill," I heard him say.

Genuine cats commit genuine deeds! EQUALITY!!

"If that's it, I'm about to go back to bed," I responded as I headed to my bedroom.

"Nigga, the only thing that you can catch while you're sleep is a dream and you ain't promise to have that," I heard him say as I walked down the hallway.

I wanted to tell him that I don't have dreams, I have visions. It's a known fact that those who have dreams also have nightmares, but that would've took us to another plane, and I wasn't energized enough for that conversation.

-TERESA-

I was sitting behind the desk looking at the pictures that me and Deamon took when we was in Charlotte when this inmate walked in holding his bandaged wrist.

"May I help you?" I asked as he approached my desk.

"My name is Marcus Jones and I just transferred from Leisburg, I was suppose to come earlier, but the officer in the dorm was tripping," he replied.

"Well, you were called earlier, but now all of the nurses are gone, so you have to come back in the morning."

"Well, do you have some type of pain medicine or something for my wrist. I was suppose to get x-rays on it?" He asked as his eyes explored my pictures.

"I'm not authorized to give you any pain medication," I stressed as I flipped the pictures over.

"Are you from around here?" Was his next question.

Now a woman gets tired of the same questions from every inmate who tries to come in here and put his mack down, so I let it be known first hand that I'm not interested.

"No, and I don't think I know you!" I responded in an agitated manner.

"I wasn't trying to say that," he responded with a light smile exposing the fact that he had gold fronts, "but the truck on that picture looks like my brother Kruger's."

Now I know he just didn't say my boo's name, and he talking about he's his brother.

"You know Deamon?" I asked in a shocked manner.

"Yeah, they call me Hammah."

"I should have known with all them pretty ass gold teeth in your mouth," I found myself lightning up on him, "please don't tell Deamon that I gave you a hard time," I added with a smile of my own.

"You alright, you ain't know."

He seemed pretty cool so I thought that I'd show him the pictures since no-one else was around.

"These are the pictures we took in Charlotte. We just got back yesterday," I stated as I gave him the mini photo album, "but he didn't tell me that you was coming here."

"Don't nobody know," he replied as he looked through the pictures with a wide grin, "I fell on my wrist playing ball the other day so they shipped me here to make sure it wasn't broken."

"He didn't tell you about me?" I found myself asking.

"We don't talk that much since I don't call home like that," he replied as he smiled at the pictures.

"When I get home I'm gonna let him know that you're here, is there anything you want me to tell him?"

"Just tell him know I'm here," he replied as he handed me the photos back.

"You can keep them, I have another book in the car, just don't show them off until you get back to Leisburg. I ain't trying to get fired," I stressed as I handed them back the photos.

"Preciate that," he responded before saying, "I hope you try to get me up here in the morning."

"I will, It was nice meeting you," I stressed as he walked towards the door.

"That goes for me too," he replied before walking out.

Now I know Deamon is gonna flip. He always talking about Hammah this and Hammah that. I done saw all the letters from him in the nightstand drawer.

I think our trip to Charlotte drew us closer. I mean, I feel by meeting my family, maybe he can understand me a little better.

All my life me and my cousins have competed on everything, especially men. So when he told me that Bambi was trying to seduce him, I couldn't trip, cause I sort of pulled the same move on her a few years back. But he handled himself right, and I really love his ass for that.

I hate the fact that his ass left me home all horny yesterday. Summer Street can't be putting out like me, but best believe I'm gonna get me some tonight. That's almost guaranteed, especially after I tell him that I met Hammah today.

****

Gunslanga sat on the couch in the living room of his trap house in the dark with Fredel. A candle was the only illumination in the house, and it sat in the middle of the coffee table. The only thing Slanga had close to him was his Glock.

"Say Slanga," Fredel stressed.

"What up?"

"You ever hear about them two little cats from the county name Lil Dusty and Baby Gotti?"

"Yeah, they was them young niggas who hit that Cuban up for that brick a while back."

"Yeah, that's them, but that nigga Lil Dusty is me and Kay-Kay's cousin."

"So what's up with him?"

"They came up off that little bit and they still buying byrds, but they really don't have nobody to cope from that's reliable."

"So who they coping from?"

"Some nigga in a burgundy vert ."

"Oh yeah!"

"You know him?" Fredel asked.

"Yeah, I know him," Gunslanga responded with a sly grin that Fredel couldn't see.

That's when he heard somebody walk on the porch before he heard Kruger stress, "Open this door fool."

The moment Kruger stepped in he turned the lights on.

"Man, what the fuck is wrong with you?!" Gunslanga practically yelled.

"Man, I ain't about to be sitting in the muthafucking dark like that!" Kruger replied as he sat next to him on the couch.

"What up Slanga?" Hamburger greeted after walking in after Kruger.

"And then you bring a big ass cheeseburger in here with you," he stressed as he slid his pistol under the cushions of the couch.

"Nigga, I know you miss me with your big bean head ass!" Hamburger stressed after sitting next to Fredel.

"What up Fredel?' Kruger greeted.

"Shit bra, just trying to get this money with big homie here," Fredel replied with a wide grin.

"Now that's what's up," Kruger stressed before taking his attention off of him and asking Gunslanga, "guess who on his way here?"

"Just tell me fool," Gunslanga snapped back.

"Vito," Kruger responded with a light smile before adding, "he say he should be here later on tonight, he in Atlanta right now."

"He don't believe in calling and letting us know ahead of time, do he?" Gunslanga questioned.

"That's the same thing I said."

"I guess we gotta show them a good time, cause I know he brought his wife with him."

"You already know."

"Yeah my nigga, after the time they showed us down there, we have to show them a good time," Gunslanga implied.

"Now that's the same thing I said," Hamburger stressed with a wide grin.

Gunslanga grabbed a pillow from the couch and threw it at Hamburger before stressing, "Ain't nobody ask you what you said!"

Hamburger threw the pillow back at him before saying, "I see you ain't gonna be happy until I beat your ass!"

"Don't worry Burger," Kruger raised over Gunslanga and stressed, "if he try anything, I got him."

Gunslanga just looked up at him and chuckled, "Man, you really don't want that."

"Jump then fool!" Kruger stressed.

Gunslanga rose up and grabbed Kruger. They tussled for a minute before Hamburger grabbed them both and slung them both back on the couch.

Hamburger then looked over at Fredel and said, "Man, this here is all the time with these fools."

Kruger raised from the couch and straightened his clothes before saying, "I gotta go and holler at Teresa before Vito get here."

"Well, when you leave there come back and scoop me up," Gunslanga stressed.

"Will do," he replied before asking Hamburger, "Is you staying down here?"

"Hell na'll," Gunslanga answered for him, "take his ass with you!"

"Man, you know I can't stay here with this fool," Hamburger stressed as he headed for the door, "I would've been beat his ass."

"Ya'll hold that shit down and turn my lights back off," Gunslanga replied as they walked out the door.

****

"Why did it take you so long to come and see me?" Phylisha was asking Weasel as she reached for the blunt he was passing.

"I told you I have an ole lady now, so dealing with her and the streets, I seldom have time for myself," he replied as he stretched out on the couch.

He could tell that this irked her a little, but he knew it wasn't a point in lying. He really didn't want to be there but he had nothing else to do with Ericka out of town visiting her peoples.

"Well, you know I have a friend too, but that's as far as it goes with me," she revealed before taking a long pull and adding, "I just can't see no nigga checking my every move."

Weasel just smirked at the comment before replying with, "See, it ain't about the nigga checking your every move. When you find somebody you wanna really be with, you tend to check yourself. I can't think of one nigga who wants a woman that his co-workers can say they had."

"Nigga you sell dope, you ain't got no job! So where the hell is your co-workers?"

"See that's where ya'll get it twisted," he responded with a sinister grin, "that just happens to be the hardest profession. I mean you can't get a grant to learn what I do, it's strictly hands on, pay your own way."

"So you saying that's your job?" She sarcastically asked.

"That's how I pay my bills, ain't it?" He sternly pointed out.

"I always wondered why niggas sell dope," she stated as she raised from the couch and headed towards her bathroom.

"Have you ever wondered why you fuck with niggas who sell dope?" He questioned in a disgusted manner.

At that moment he wondered why he was even there in the first place. He had obviously forgot how she acted, but he noticed that she didn't mind refreshing his memory. He thought back to the day he met her in the mall, and realized that it was never her that appealed to him, it was her cool as son, Lil Mark.

"Where Lil Mark at?" He asked after realizing that he hadn't seen him.

"He's at his grandmother's house," he heard her reply from the bedroom.

The thing that tripped him out was why did she have the water running in the hall bathroom, but she was in her bedroom. He stopped everything he was doing and keened in on any other sounds from the back and that's when he heard her whispering.

Something told him to grab the phone that sat on the coffee table, but he knew that he couldn't just pick it up without her knowing, so he did the first thing that came to his mind.

"Say Phylisha," he called out.

When she answered him he picked up the phone and placed his hand over the receiver.

"Do you think you can bring me a cup of ice on your way back in here?"

"You know I got you," she yelled back before he heard her talking to some cat on the phone.

"You see what I'm talking about?" She stressed to the guy.

The voice on the other end said, "Just keep the nigga occupied for a minute and me and the fellas coming through."

Death was the only word that could describe the expression on Weasel's face. Something told him to just get up and leave, but his pride wouldn't allow him to budge. He also knew that she had done gave them the scoop on him so if they wouldn't get him tonight, they were definitely going to be looking for him in the near future, and he just couldn't leave knowing that. He hung up the phone the moment she did.

"Dam baby girl, what's taking you so long with that ice?" He asked in a frustrated manner.

He heard when the water stopped running an she walked back in with an attitude, "Dam, can a bitch use the bathroom?"

"I hope that you at least washed your hands," he implied.

She stopped at the kitchen doorway and rolled her eyes at him before stressing, "I ain't like that!"

"I ain't say you was," he responded as he rose from the couch and followed her to the kitchen.

He walked right behind her as she was washing the glass out and grabbed her hips from behind.

"Weasey," she moaned out, "you know I can't concentrate with you touching me like that."

She wore a sky blue pull over gown that stopped in the middle of her thick thighs. He slid his hand under her night gown and gently squeezed her breast, causing her to drop the glass in the sink.

195

STILL STUCK

He then took his other hand and slipped it through the seams of her thongs. When his fingers dropped a little further, he couldn't help but smile, because she was already moist. With no hesitation, he dipped two of his fingers in the foils of her pussy causing her to whimper.

After a few moments of him sliding his fingers in and out of her he eased them out and placed them in her mouth.

"Now I remember why I fuck with you," he whispered in her ear with a smile of approval.

She turned around and faced him before she asked, "And why is that?"

"You already know," he replied as he scooped her up in his arms.

"I thought you said you wanted a cup of ice?" She sarcastically giggled out.

"I'll come back and get it myself," he stated as he carried her to the bedroom.

After placing her on the bed he snatched two head scarves from the dresser.

"What you gonna do with them?" She asked with a lustful expression.

Either she was too sexually aroused or she was a good actress, because he saw no signs of deceit.

"I thought we would change it up a little," he responded before grabbing her wrist and tying them to the head board.

When he was content with the knots, he walked out of the room.

"Where you going?" She asked with a look of anticipation.

"I'll be right back," he replied without breaking his stride.

He quietly stepped out of the apartment and walked to his car. After popping the trunk, he grabbed the bag he had twenty grand in, his .45 and a 9mm.

When he stepped back in the apartment he made sure he locked the door behind him. He then walked back in the kitchen and grabbed a knife and the glass of ice. On his way to the bedroom he grabbed the bottle of *Hennessy* he'd left on the coffee table.

"Dam nigga, what you plan on doing with that knife?" She asked after he stepped in and threw the bag next to the bed.

"You ain't scared, is you?" He questioned with a cold expression as he poured him a glass of cognac.

After finishing his drank he grabbed the knife and cut her night gown and thongs off.

She gasped before stressing, "Now, you know that you have to buy me some more."

"You wanna run this show or are you gonna let me make this shit happen?" He asked as he paused for a moment and looked her over.

She had a nice body with a neatly shaved patch over her pussy. For a moment he couldn't believe that this same sexy ass woman was trying to end his life for nothing. He then walked over to the bag and pulled the two pistols and placed them under the far pillow.

Phylisha just laid there in silence as he started undressing.

"Is this what you want?" He asked her as he slid two condoms on.

She really didn't know what he was talking about due to it being so dark in the room, but as soon as he crawled over her as stiff as a log, she responded.

"You know it is," she managed to whimper out as he teased the foils of her pussy with the tip of his dick.

Out of nowhere he drove into her with massive force, "Is this what you wanted bitch?!"

She was too caught up in the moment to respond. She was so flushed with so many different sensations that she almost instantly exploded. Weasel noticed that her body went limp and grabbed the knife again. After cutting her hands free, he placed her on her hands and knees.

As he entered her from the back he held no pity. From the sounds she was making along with the constant slapping of their bodies, he knew that he was giving her the ride of her life. He continued to pound in and out of her as he slapped her hard on her ass cheeks, over and over again.

She bent over to bite on the sheets but he grabbed her hair and pulled her back.

"Na'll bitch, let me hear you scream!" He demanded through clinched teeth.

She attempted to meet his every stroke, but she always seem to be just a half a second late, so he was able to go a little deeper.

199

"Weasel please," she managed to stutter out.

"It's a little too late for that!" He replied with a vengeance.

In the mist of him pounding her from the back he heard a knock at the door.

She looked back at him as he slid out of her and laid over the pillow he'd hid the guns under and said, "I don't wanna answer that."

"At least see who it is," he encouraged, "that might be Lil Mark."

She then raised from the bed and put her house coat on before walking towards the front door. When Weasel heard the front door open he walked into the living room with a pair of boxers on and both pistols in hand. He hid in the shadows for a moment until he heard the front door close.

"Now ain't this some shit!" He stated with a sly grin that was barely visible because of the lack of light as he held the two pistols at her and the three assailants she had just let in.

"What's wrong Weasel?" She asked in a terrified manner.

He paid her no attention and stayed focused on the dudes.

"Say fellas, I need ya'll to unleash ya'll guns and maybe I won't have to unleash some of this hot lead," he practically commanded as he waved the .45 towards the couch.

Weasel saw that one of them decided to move so he stressed, "Now, before you pull that thing all the way out, just make sure you're content on what you wanna do."

The guy grabbed the wooden grip of his 357 and placed it on the coffee table.

"Dave, what you got that for?" Phylisha asked while moving towards Weasel.

"Bitch, if you don't step back over there, you'll turn into Toni Braxton, cause your ass will never breath again!" Weasel stressed.

"But Weasel," she began to plea.

"I know, just get over there," he replied in a cold manner.

"Man, this my cousin," the guy she identified as Dave said, "I was just coming through and checking on her."

"So you just decided to roll through, out the muthafucking blue?" Weasel questioned before revealing, "Man, it's dam near midnight!"

Weasel paid him no further attention and focused on the other two assailants. One of them looked as if he was itching to make a move.

"Now look at you," Weasel said to him, "you fighting like a muthafucka to be the first to catch it. Now, if ya'll have some heat, you ain't got but five seconds to put it on it table."

With all of the lights out in the house they could barely make out his body let alone his facial expression so instead of trying their luck, they did what they were told.

"Now, all of ya'll strip!" He demanded before looking over at Phylisha and saying, "Yeah, you too."

"But I didn't do anything!" She frantically whined out as she walked towards him.

When she was in arm reach he slapped her hard to the ground with the .45 before stating, "Bitch, you done called these niggas to come and rob and probably kill me, and you still claiming you ain't did shit!"

With no hesitation he kicked her in the stomach, "Now take that shit off!"

After they were all naked, he ordered them into the child's room, tied them up and closed the door. He could hear them whispering about something as he wiped down everything he felt he had touched. When he was satisfied with everything, he got dressed, grabbed his bag and was headed out the door.

He was just about to walk out, but thought about it and stepped back in. When he walked back in the child's room he pulled the 357 that Dave put on the table, and put a hole in each of their heads, giving Phylisha the extra one.

****

"Wake up playboy!" Gunslanga was knocking on Kruger's bedroom door with Vito next to him giggling.

"Say cuz-o," Vito stressed, "why you sleeping so late?"

Deidra shook him and whispered, "Deamon, Vito and Slanga at the door."

"What time is it?" He asked her.

"It's only 10:15," she replied before throwing the comforter over her head.

"Man, if you don't get your ass up!" Gunslanga stressed.

"I'm coming, dam man, I'm coming!" He responded as he slid out of bed and headed towards the door.

When he opened the door he stressed, "Dam, I might as well still be locked up if ya'll gonna wake a playa up every morning for inspection."

"Dam nigga, what you trying to get your beauty sleep or something?" Vito joked.

"The nigga sleep like that every morning," Gunslanga interjected.

"No I don't!" Kruger retorted, "Cause you wake me up dam near every morning with this bullshit!"

They bickered back and forth as they walked in the living room. Kruger then realized that him and Deidra was the only ones still in bed, because Larissa and Amanda was sitting on the couch.

"They got ya'll up this early too?" Kruger asked them with sympathy.

"Me and Vito always up early," Larissa revealed.

"And you know that fool won't let me sleep if he can help it," Amanda added.

Kruger noticed that they were all dressed and about to head out somewhere so he asked, "Where ya'll about to go?"

"Grab some breakfast from somewhere," Amanda replied.

"Well, ya'll gotta at least give us a minute to get dressed," he insisted as he headed back to the room.

A few hours later they had split up in two separate vehicles. The girls were in Vito's rental truck while the fellas were in Kruger's truck.

"So what's the word cuz-o?" Kruger asked Vito.

"I just got a few heads to chop off in Atlanta," Vito replied as if this was an everyday conversation for him.

"What, somebody done tried to bite the hand that feed them?" Gunslanga questioned.

"Yeah, they tried us with some counterfeit," Vito replied with a frustrated expression.

"How much?" Kruger asked.

"A quarter mill."

"Off with they muthafucking heads then!" Gunslanga stressed with aggression.

"I know right," Vito agreed with a light smile.

"You need some help?" Kruger asked.

Vito's face brighten up before he replied with, "Man, I'm glad you asked me before I asked you."

"Well I'm riding too," Gunslanga stressed from the backseat.

"Na'll, big homie," Kruger stressed, "you already got your shine on without me in Savannah. So right now I'm playing catch up. Besides, one of us has to be here, anything could go wrong."

"So when ya'll riding out?" Gunslanga asked in a disappointed manner.

"Since it's just us two, we can head out tomorrow morning and be back by tomorrow night. I got everything we need in Atlanta, so we ain't gotta ride dirty," Vito replied.

"Say no more," Kruger replied with a sinister expression.

✳✳✳✳✳✳✳✳✳✳✳✳✳✳✳

Jimmy sat on the edge of the bed watching the news while Surina was in the bathroom. He'd picked a nervous Weasel up the previous night from a gas station and took him to the 13th Street bridge to throw a pistol in the river, so he knew that Weasel had done something. Just as he suspected, four bodies had been found, so he turned the volume up.

"Four bodies were found in an apartment building off of Kissingbower Road. Phylisha Jenkins was found in her apartment along with three men. It appears to be an execution styled murder."

There was more said about the killings but that was all Jimmy heard before he said, "Dam Weasel."

Just so happen, Surina was coming out of the bathroom when he said that to himself.

"What has Weasel done now?" Surina asked as she stood over him.

The look on his face must have answered the question because she implied, "I know Weasel ain't kill them people?"

"What the fuck is you talking about?" He stressed in an aggravated manner, "You need to go sit your ass down! How the fuck is you gonna come out your mouth with some shit like that?!"

She was dumbfounded as she looked down at him. If she was just speculating at first, his reaction told her that her speculation was right on point. At that moment she hated the fact that she was so open and direct, she wished that she had kept her mouth shut, but instead of falling apart she tried a different approach.

"Jimmy, you're getting a little too off the chain for me, I'll holler at you a little later," she stressed as she started putting on her shoes.

"You know what," he responded as he rose from the bed, "that sounds like a good idea. But let me tell you an even better one," he added with a sinister grin, "don't bring your dumb ass back!"

The expression on her face told him that she didn't give a dam one way or the other, so he decided to add a little extras.

"And when you get on post tell Travis I said what up," he stressed with a smirk, "maybe he can eat that pussy a little better than I do."

Her facial expression changed up from satisfied to confused almost instantly. She wanted to ask him how he knew anything about Travis, but instead she wanted him to feel just as silly as he had just made her feel.

Before she walked out the door she turned and stated, "Maybe if you had a future in what you do, I wouldn't have to go on post to see Travis."

She obviously knew he would snap on her after her rebuttal because she immediately slammed the door shut. Not even a second later, she heard something hit the door and shatter, causing her to walk away feeling victorious.

Jimmy laid on the bed with heavier things on his mind, than Surina. He wanted to call Weasel and scream on him, but he knew his words would go in one ear and out the other.

Everything in his life had turned from a smooth Infiniti ride to a complete roller coaster, and at that moment the only thing that eased him a little was hustling.

-KRUGER-

"Man, Uncle Benny be trying to sho-nuff hit a playa with that preaching thing," Vito was saying.

"Man, that's every time he see me. That's why I don't go through there too funny," I replied as I was driving towards the apartment so he could see Tamika.

Teresa has been hitting me up for one reason or the other, but Lord knows that I ain't in no rush to see her, not after the week we just spent together. I was suppose to go by there last night, but I got caught up with Diedra.

"Some of that shit he was spitting was real though," Vito continued with a sincere look.

"Man, I already know where you're going with that," I replied before he started feeling like he was on the pulpit.

"But it's real cousin," he rebutted, "we have to make a change some day, cause it ain't no way that we can keep living like this."

Lord knows that I feel him in every way. It's so much that's going on in my everyday life. Hell, that's probably why it be so hard for me to get out of bed in the morning. If it wasn't for the realities of life and the people GOD has placed in my cipher to keep me strong, I'd probably say it fuck it too.

"You know I wanta be able to come home to my wife and kids in a business suit one day," I heard cuz-o say.

"Look playboy, I think about that myself from time to time, but right now I'm caught up in the middle of a lot of bullshit. I have too many people depending on me to just jump out like that," I found myself saying.

Cuz-o looked over at me with one of those sly grins before saying, "You know I can feel you on that. Hell, I'm down there with nothing but phony ass family and when they want something, who do you think they call?"

I deserved that.

"But what I'm saying is," he continued, "I'm tired of being the one who take all the risk

211

to help a bunch of muthafuckas who I know won't take the time to send me a card if I was to get locked-up."

Now he's talking my language.

"Man, I just did a bid myself, and I received a few letters here and there from a few family members, so I know exactly where you coming from."

He nodded his head to let me know he understood.

"All that did was show me that if I don't get out here and get it, it ain't nann nigga gonna get it for me. Besides, we just happen to be the type of cats people lean on."

"I can dig that cousin, but you have to realize that if it wasn't for Larissa, I'll be straight naked out here."

"I know you ain't talking financially?" I implied.

"Na'll cuz-o, I'm good on that. I'm speaking more on the level of having a real purpose of being here. It's a blessing to wake up next to somebody who ain't always concerned about what you can do for them."

"Well, that makes two of us," I replied with a smile of approval.

"That's how I know what Uncle Benny was screaming was real," he stated with a smile of his own.

Me and Slanga always kicking it like this, Burger too. I guess I didn't realize that I had some blood with similar traits as us. Having someone you can view life with is a helluva perk out here. It ain't enough of us sitting down and analyzing things like this, that's the main reason genuine muthafuckas are losing out here.

When we finally walked in the apartment, Tamika was in her usual spot with her books wide open. You gotta love her for that. When she saw Vito, I thought she was gonna have her baby, she was screaming so loud.

I let them do their thing while I stepped in the back and checked on Teresa. Here she is laying on the bed with that funky ass look.

"Now, what's wrong with you?" I had to ask.

"I've been trying to get in touch with you forever! It's like that now, where you just don't answer my calls no more?" She sadly questioned, "You know I could've been in the hospital or something."

And she's right, I just wasn't thinking on that level, so she has me dead to the wrong.

"My bad baby-girl," I responded in a more suave manner as I laid next to her, "Vito came in town and I guess I lost my mind. Do you forgive me?"

She tried to play hard, but I saw a smile creep in before she stressed, "Guess who I met yesterday and saw this morning?"

Now I really wasn't in the mood for the guessing game, but with me being in the wrong already, this is the hand I've just been dealt.

"Who, some serial killer?"

"No crazy," she managed to giggle out, "I met Hammah."

"Hammah who?"

"Your Hammah," she responded as she sat up, "the same Hammah you always talking about."

"Stop playing so much," I stated as I sat up.

"Baby, I know how you feel about him," she stated with a sincere expression, "I wouldn't play with you like that."

"What the hell he doing there?"

"He hurt his wrist playing basketball."

"Is he alright?"

"He was suppose to get checked today, but the x-ray machine was down."

"That's my brother right there!" I stated with excitement .

"That's what he said."

"You gotta take something to him for me," I let her know.

"What is it?"

Now I know she know what time it is, but if she wants to play crazy, who am I to get in the way of that.

"Don't worry about it, just make sure he gets it. I'll have it wrapped up so you won't know."

"I'll make sure he gets it, but you better not be getting me fired," she stated in a joking manner.

215

I just smiled at this before I told her to come up front and meet Vito.

****

Gunslanga sat on the couch talking with Fredel, Lil Dusty and Baby Gotti.

"Look Slanga," Baby Gotti was saying, "ya'll doing your thing and all, and we respect that. But all me and Dust looking for is somebody we can rely on when it's time for us to ree-up."

There wasn't a lot of people who could grasp Gunslanga's attention the way these two had. He secretly admired how they carried their selves.

"So what ya'll looking to get?" He finally asked in a nonchalant manner.

"If you can get a good number, we can leave here with two right now," Lil Dusty eagerly answered.

"The best price I can do right now is 28."

"We good with that," Baby Gotti assured with a sly grin.

Gunslanga gave the two youngster a slight smile as he nodded his head before turning to Fredel, "Tell Kay-Kay to bring two out here."

"Look," he added after Fredel walked out of the room, "I have to charge ya'll that right now, cause we down to our last. But if you spend like you claim, it ain't no way that I can keep taxing ya'll like that, feel me?"

Both of them looked at each other and smiled before Lil Dusty responded with, "Now that's the business!"

Kay-Kay came out of the back with a bag and handed it to Gunslanga who eventually handed it to Lil Dusty. Baby Gotti took his back pack off, took his pistol and two grand out of it before handing it to Kay-Kay.

"What up cuz-o?" Lil Dusty greeted her.

"Nothing really," she replied with a sly grin, "But I see you still doing you."

"I'm the only one who really know how to do me," he responded with a wide grin.

Gunslanga sat back and attentively watched everyone with smiles on their faces before, "Ya'll be safe out there and Kay-Kay and

217

Fredel make sure they make it to their ride alright."

"True that," Fredel responded without thinking nothing of it, while Kay-Kay gave him a suspicious expression.

Gunslanga paid her no attention as he watched them walk out the door. He was disgusted with the fact that they would allow their youngest cousin to get more money than them. After wrestling with that thought for a moment, he came to the conclusion that everybody can't see the bigger picture.

(CHAPTER 6)

Kruger sat in the passenger seat of Vito's rental truck as they rode down I-20, headed towards Atlanta. The sounds of Trick Daddy's, *'Back In The Days'*, blasted through the factory speakers and Kruger was reciting the lyrics word for word.

"Dam cuz," Vito stated as he turned the music down, "I didn't know that you was on that Trick like that."

Kruger looked over at him with an expression that said, "How can I not be on a nigga who spitting like bra!"

"My bad cuz," Vito managed to chuckle.

"You know, I've been thinking about cranking up a record company or something on that level," Kruger revealed after a brief moment.

"So, what you waiting on?"

"That shit just calls for too much time right now, and that's just something I'm all in on these days."

"Fuck that my folk!" Vito retorted, "If you think that your time is snatched up now, just wait until both of your girls drop them loads."

Kruger looked over at his older cousin, "I never thought about that."

After seeing his look of confusion, Vito stated, "But I know that it's nothing to a trooper. I mean, I take care of mine and I don't even like my baby mama."

"How does Larissa take it when she comes around?"

"Man, like I told you before, Larissa a soldier," he replied with a sly grin, "but on top of all that, she knows that I'm not about to fuck up what we have for my baby mama."

"That's respect," Kruger replied as he looked out of the window.

"You know me and Ron rode around and did a little catching up. I came to realize that cuz got a strong mind," Vito stressed.

"Yeah," Kruger agreed as he looked at the road ahead of them, "he really trying to do the right thing, that's why I stay out of his way. I don't want the dirt I do today, alter what happens to him tomorrow."

"Now, that's love right there," Vito assured with a smile of approval.

"Man, if I had another chance to do it all over, I'd probably go the same route bra is going. But on a genuine aspect, when I look at my life, I'm sort of content with most of the choices I made. I mean, at the least, I learned from the negative and built a stronger positive."

Vito glanced over at Kruger and couldn't help but smile. When they were younger, he always wonder what life had in store for him. He had to admit that he had his doubts about Kruger, but just hearing the way his mind traveled, he knew that he would be all good.

"So what's the plan when we get in Atlanta?" Kruger asked.

"Man, this a simple hit. I could've done it myself, but it ain't nothing like having another trooper to put in work with you."

"See, it's like six of these cats in Decatur. Now, they're either in one or two locations, but they're almost always together."

"You say you have everything we need?"

"Yeah, I got a couple vest, choppers and a few pistols. I even got a grenade launcher if we need it."

This seem to excite Kruger because he sat erect in his seat before stating, "Dam cuz, you ain't bullshitting!"

"This is what I do my folk," he replied with a light smile, "I get paid to take muthafuckas heads off when they violate the family. And since you're with me, we split the earnings 50/50."

"I'll tell you what, you just give me twenty percent and buy lunch and we straight. Reason being, I don't do this for cheese, I do it on the principle. Besides, I need to release some stress," Kruger replied with a wide grin as he reclined his seat back.

-TERESA-

Now Deamon knows that his ass is dead wrong! The things I do for this muthafuckin nigga! I have to be the slowest bitch on this side of the Mississippi. This nigga got me trafficking drugs into this prison.

Now here my dumb ass is putting my job on the line for his ass. But to top all of that, he want me to sneak him my cell-phone too! I don't even suppose to have my phone in the building! The things I do for his ass. He has to know that he has a lot of making up to do for this here.

I just called Hammah up here since it's close to count time. He can stay during count and use the phone in the bathroom. I just hope that he ain't down in that dorm running his mouth, cause Lord knows I don't need that heat.

"What's up Ms. Davis?" Hammah greeted as he walked through the door.

"Hey Mr. Jones, how are you doing?"

"A little better than I was last week," he replied before implying, "but I was wondering who the girl in the white dress was on them photos."

How comes everybody likes Nicole's dingy ass? "That's my cousin Nicole," I replied in a dull manner.

"She like that?" He asked with a disappointed expression.

I just nodded my head.

"I mean, I wasn't looking to marry her or nothing like that," he stated, "I was just looking for someone who don't mind corresponding with a nigga."

"You sound just like Deamon," I found myself saying, "she's a lawyer, but I'll try to hook you up."

"That's up," he replied with a sly grin, "but have you talked to bra yet?"

"Yeah, and he gave me something to give you," I stated as I heard that it was count time over my radio.

That's when I raised up from my desk and walked in the inmates bathroom. After I put everything by the trash can, I walked back out.

"Walk in there, look next to the trash can and grab all that shit ya'll niggas got me risking my job for. The other fools number is on that piece of paper, call him while you're in there," I instructed his ass before I made my way back to my desk.

I watched as his ass grinned from ear to ear all the way in the bathroom, and I couldn't help but smile myself. It actually made me feel good knowing that I could make him and my boo smile for the day.

****

Weasel was laying on the couch with two bottles of Hennessy on the floor next to him. One was empty while the other one was a little over half full. He'd just got off the phone with Jimmy who was now on his way over, but Weasel wasn't in the mood to converse with anyone.

Mixed with disappointment and rage he couldn't bring himself to do anything but smoke and drank. The fact that he kept putting himself in so many life or death situations had disturbed him more than he'd wish to admit.

When he thought of Phylisha and her team of goons it never felt wrong until he thought of her son, that just made him drank even more.

"I mean, what was I supposed to do?!" He screamed out in a slurred manner before he heard the knock at the door.

"Who is it?" He managed to slur out.

"Man, open this dam door!" Jimmy demanded.

Weasel had to struggle to rise off the couch. When he finally opened the door, the sun blinded him.

"Dam nigga!" Jimmy stated as he grabbed him to guide him back to the couch, "You need to slow down on that oil."

"I know right," he replied with a look of defeat.

"Bra, you got this shit smelling like a liquor barrel!" He stressed as he closed and locked the front door, "Ericka is gonna kill your ass if you don't get this shit together."

Weasel jerked a little bit before he ended up vomiting on himself.

"Dam!" Jimmy spat out, "Man, why the fuck you wait until I get over here to do some shit like that?!"

Jimmy walked in the kitchen and grabbed a few towels from the counter and tried to wipe most of the vomit off the couch, but all he managed to do was smear it.

"Man, we have to get you out of here before you lose the little bit of sanity you got left!" Jimmy stressed as he helped him to the bathroom.

-KRUGER-

Here we are sitting in a green Grand Am waiting for these cats to make an appearance and cuz is on the phone with Larissa playing hubby. It amazes me how he can be the perfect executioner and the perfect courtier all in the same hour.

I just got off the phone with Deidra, cause she was over there feeling neglected. How can I blame her with Larissa talking on the phone with Vito and Amanda talking on the phone with Slanga. She's home base now, so she must be treated as such. That's some shit Vito keeps screaming in my ear.

"Yo cuz," I stated as I saw this cat come out the house.

"Man, don't you see me on the phone with my wife!" He blasted back.

This cat be really tripping when it comes down to her. Whatever she has between her legs got his ass delirious.

"Nigga dam that!" I snapped back, "Is that one of them cats right there?"

"My time to shine sweet heart," is all this fool says before he hangs the phone up.

"Yo cuz," he called out as he opened the passenger door, "don't move until I call you."

Now out of all the things to say to me, he instructs me to stay put. Despite my true feelings, I did what I was told. This was his show, I was just co-starring.

I watched him walk towards buddy, while he was at the mail box, and pull his pistol out. I guess, if you have to get somebody, and you really want to get them, it doesn't matter one way or the other if you get them in broad daylight and out in the open.

"Check and see if I have any mail in there," I clearly heard Vito say to him.

Now either ole boy recognized cuz-o or the pistol had him tantalized, but buddy eyes got so big that I thought they were gonna just ooze out of the sockets.

"Man, I didn't have shit to do with that," he managed to stutter out.

"Lets just go in the house and talk about it," Vito calmly said to him as he waved the huge .44 in the direction of the house.

Moments later I watched Vito push him through the front door. Now I'm out here in this car trying to figure out my next move. It wasn't until like three or four minutes later that my phone rang.

"Yeah, what up?"

"Bring that bag off the backseat," is all he said before the line went dead.

When I walked through the front door, I couldn't help but admire how elegant and spacious these cats house was. It really made me think twice about dealing with that dogg food. After I walked through the living room and into the dining area, I saw Vito standing over buddy as he sat in one of the dinner chairs.

"You don't ask the questions, that's my part. It's your job to answer them," he stated as if he was having a casual conversation.

After seeing me and the look on Vito's face, buddy just nodded his head in agreement.

"So where your homeboys at?" Vito asked.

"Who are you talking," buddy started to ask right before Vito slapped him hard across the face with the .44, causing blood to instantly run down his cheeks as if he'd just poured water on his face.

"Look man, I really didn't wanta do that," Vito stated in this calm manner that I wasn't accustomed to hearing at times like this, "But I could have sworn I told you your part."

Cuz-o had this mad scientist type of demeanor that took me to another dimension, so I could only imagine what buddy was feeling.

"Alright man, dam, alright!" He screamed as he placed his hand over his wound.

"So where they at?" Cuz-o asked again.

"They should be on their way here," he replied.

Vito looked back at me with this sinister grin that had me feeling like the target. I watched as he put the Desert Eagle to buddy head and squeezed the trigger twice. The impact from the .44 forced his body to flip backwards and he fell to the ground slumped over the chair.

"Man, you ain't even ask him where they got that boy stashed at!" I stressed as I walked over and appraised the head shots.

"Fool, I'm trying to get back to my baby in one piece, dam that dope," I heard him spat out as he grabbed the bag from me.

As I looked down at buddy's head I realized that he didn't have one anymore. He was definitely having a closed casket. I looked over at Vito who was fishing through the bag. He pulled out another clip to the his pistol and walked back in the front room.

"Man, I'm about to find that dope!" I stressed loud enough for him to hear me.

"Typical drug dealer," I heard him spat out.

I went and grabbed a pair of the gloves out of the bag and started searching everything. After I checked all the spots where I felt they could hide it in the kitchen, I knew that if it was in the house, it had to be in one of the bedrooms. It wasn't even five minutes later that I found it in the mini fridge of the master bedroom.

When I made my way to the front room where Vito was playing the grim reaper, I held the duffle bag up and stressed, "I told you that I'll find this boy!"

"Sssshhh," he hissed at me with his finger to his lips, "they just pulled up in two Escalades."

"Are they strapped?" I asked as I pulled out the Desert Eagle from the seams of my jeans.

"Not visibly, but you never know, so stay prepared."

"Here," I stated as I threw him my Desert Eagle, "now you're prepared."

I rushed back to the bag and pulled out two Remington .45's, "Now I'm prepared," I whispered to myself as I cocked them both.

When I stepped in the front room, Vito motioned that they were at the front door, so I eased on the other side of the front room entrance. All I had to do was peep around the corner and I had a full view of the front door. Vito was hiding behind the huge couch, so we were gonna hit them from both angles.

"Wait until they are all inside," he whispered as I heard the dead bolt unlock.

They obviously wasn't aware of what was about to go down cause they were laughing and joking about something. The moment the last cat stepped through the door, I heard Vito's Desert Eagle's erupt. When I showed my hand it was all over for them dudes. We ranged so many shots in them that you would think that we were playing an arcade game.

Some how the first guy managed to escape towards the dining room nursing his stomach, so I knew it was on me to feed him his demise. I took my time as I trailed him. When I caught up with him, he had a chair and was about to throw it through the bay window. That's when I raised the .45 in my right hand and squeezed the trigger over and over. His body collapsed over his friend who Vito had clipped earlier.

"I'll give you whatever you want," he had the nerve to say to me with blood oozing out of his mouth.

Man, I know I just put like six holes in this fool and he still breathing.

"We already got that playboy," I found myself saying as I put the nose of the pistol in my left hand to his eye and squeezed the trigger.

"Make sure you grab everything and come on out," Vito stressed from the doorway before he walked out.

I put my pistols back in the bag, and grabbed it and the dogg food. When I walked out towards the rental car, Vito was messing around in the trunk.

I looked around and realized that the neighborhood was just as peaceful as it was when we first drove through ninety minutes earlier. When I stepped to the trunk I noticed that Vito was loading the grenade launcher.

"You said that you wanted to see what kind of damage it made," he implied with a sly grin as he pulled it out and handed it to me.

"Dam right!" I excitedly replied.

"You remember when Uncle Vernon use to take us in the woods and let us shot?" He asked.

I just nodded my head as I appraised the launcher.

"You remember what he use to tell us?"

"Yeah," I replied as I looked up at him, "don't tell our mama's, cause they'll be mad at him."

Vito just burst out laughing before stressing, "Not that part, the other part nigga. You

234

remember he said that you only have one shot, so make sure you hit what you're aiming at."

"True, true, true," I managed to chuckle out.

I raised it on my shoulder and pointed it at the front door. When I pulled the trigger, it made me jerk a little to the side. It wasn't that it had a helluva kick, I think that I was just anticipating a more heavier one. So instead of hitting the front door, the grenade hit the side of the house and exploded.

I stood there for a moment as the dust and things cleared up and realized that I now could see through the house.

I must had stood there a moment too long because I heard Vito stress, "What you trying to do, win an Oscar or something, bring your ass on!"

****

Weasel and Jimmy were riding through the city with the sounds of 2-Pac's, *'It Ain't Easy'*, humming through the speakers of the Infiniti.

235

Weasel had the passenger seat reclined so that he could look up into the sky through the moon roof.

"You alright playboy?" Jimmy asked.

Weasel looked over at him with a glare in his eyes, "I just gotta clear my head."

Jimmy passed him the blunt he was puffing on and turned the music up a little louder. Weasel leaned over and backed the track up, before looking over at Jimmy with a sly grin.

"I can feel you playboy," Jimmy stated with a smile of approval, "It ain't easy being me either."

Jimmy thought about Surina as he drove down Laney-Walker Boulevard. He knew that she was spending a lot of time with her soldier friend, but to his surprise, it really didn't bother him as much as he thought it would. Besides, he had his own thing going on with this Paine college senior.

Just the thought of her brought a smile to his face. She was about to be an accountant, and without her knowing it, she was already giving him a lot of ideas about cleaning his money up.

Weasel looked over at him as he turned on Summer Street and couldn't help but notice the wide grin, "Dam fool, what you grinning like that for?"

Jimmy glanced over as he pulled in Gurley's parking lot and replied with, "I'm just tripping off this little breezy I met from Paine."

"Surina gonna kill your ass," Weasel chuckled out.

"Man, me and Surin a just fuck," he replied with a cold stare right before he noticed Red and Pimp walking out the store.

Either Weasel didn't care about what had happened between the two of them or he just didn't want to get on that level at the moment. Instead he instructed Jimmy to creep up next to Red and Pimp.

The moment Jimmy pulled up to them unnoticed, Weasel jumped out of the passenger seat and yelled, "Lay it down muthafuckas!"

Red stood strong while Pimp reached in his pants.

"See, that's how niggas get killed on humbugs!" Pimp stressed after regaining his composure.

"So you ready like that cuzo?" Weasel asked as Jimmy was parking the car.

"Dam that nigga," Red stepped in and embraced Weasel, "what's up my nigga."

"Shit really, I'm just out here catching some fresh air," Weasel replied as Jimmy walked towards them.

"Well, you know that we all about that paper today, it's Friday," Pimp stressed with a gruesome expression.

Weasel could tell that his cousin was still sour about him cutting him off, but at the moment he could really care less, "Well, I'm surprised to see you out here," is all he replied with.

"Fuck what you heard, I'm all about this cheddar, playboy!" Pimp replied with authority.

Red obviously felt the animosity in the air and asked Jimmy, "What ya'll trying to get straight or something?"

Weasel cut Jimmy off and answered, "I told ya'll that we just out bending a few corners."

"Where Kruger at?" Jimmy asked surprising the other three.

Neither one of them knew that he had developed his own relationship with Kruger before he had went to Charlotte. They both decided to never let a woman get in the path of making money.

"Ain't no telling," Pimp replied.

"If you wanted to hollar at him, you know he'll answer that phone," Red assured him.

"Na'll, a nigga just wanted to speak," Jimmy replied as they walked towards 1122.

"Is Slanga still down the street?" Weasel asked.

"Yeah, he should be," Red answered.

"Well, I'm about to walk down there and see what's up with him," Weasel stressed as he walked past 1122 with Jimmy right behind him.

Just as they were crossing the four way crossing of Summer and Hopkins Street, two detective cars shot past them and headed towards Gunslanga's trap. When they looked further down, they noticed that three sheriff cars had already pulled in front of the trap. Red and Pimp caught up with Weasel and Jimmy and they all rushed to the scene.

When they reached the scene, the detectives were bringing Gunslanga out in handcuffs. They rushed him to the backseat of one of their cars and quickly speeded off. Kay-Kay stepped out of the house with her arms folded and tears flowing down her cheeks.

"Come here Kay-Kay," Red called her.

All of the police were now leaving with smiles as she walked over to Red.

"Did they find anything?" He asked as he wrapped his arms around her.

She shook her head before saying, "I don't think they was looking for nothing but him."

"He straight then," he revealed as she rested her head on his chest, "he'll beat them other charges, so stop crying."

"Slanga told me to call Kruger and let him know," she stressed as she pulled away from him.

"I'll call and let him know," Red assured her as he walked towards the front door of the house, "you just make sure you get this house clean, just in case Honeycutt and his clan swing through."

She just nodded her head as he walked her in the house.

With all of the commotion the scene had accumulated a small crowd, so when Red walked out he realized that they were still looking on.

"Everything is everything, it ain't nobody dead yet!" He stressed to the admirers with a cold stare, "Now, if that's what ya'll want, stay out here with your noses in somebody else's business!"

"This my hood youngblood!" A guy screamed from the crowd, "I was born and raised out here, so you can't tell me shit! Hell, I done did bids behind this shit here!"

"So you OG?" Red asked as he walked towards him with a devilish grin.

"Hell yeah, and it's best you recognize that!" The tall slim cat replied as the rest of the crowd distanced themselves from him.

"If you were OG, you would know when to mind your own!" Red stressed as they were face to face, "But if you have a problem with that there, we might need to handle that right now!"

Without another word spoken the guy swung on Red with his right. Red swiftly ducked the blow and upper-cutted him with his right elbow, causing the guy to bite his tongue and instantly breaking his jaw. When he fell to the ground whimpering with his hand over his mouth,

Pimp rushed over and kicked him twice in the stomach.

"You would think that somebody would have put you on point, with you being an OG and all," Pimp spat out before he spit on the guy.

****

"You gotta be bullshitting!" Kruger stressed through the receiver.

"I wish I was playboy, but I ain't," Red replied.

Kruger and Vito were in the rental truck headed back to Augusta when Red called.

"Man, I'm gonna call you back," Kruger stressed, "I have to hit the house up."

Moments later he was on the phone with Deidra. He knew that Gunslanga couldn't stay free forever, but he never thought that he'd get trapped so quick. He was now wishing he'd brought Gunslanga along on this hit. Now he was left with the responsibility of letting Amanda know.

"Baby-girl, I need to holler at Amanda," he said to Deidra.

He heard her call out her name before she finally got on the phone.

"Yeah, what's up?" She sounded as if she was having a good time.

"You know I hate to be the one to tell you this, but they just locked Slanga up."

"For what?" She replied in a humble manner.

"Those warrants."

The phone was silent for a moment before she asked, "So what he need me to do?"

Kruger just smiled because he knew that she was willing to do whatever for her man.

"I don't know just yet, but he should be calling the house within the hour, so don't go nowhere, cause you know he gonna want to talk to you."

"Alright," she almost whispered, "do you wanna speak back to Deidra?"

"If you don't mind."

A few moments past before Deidra picked the phone back up, "So what do you want me to do?"

"I can't call it, just make sure she alright," he replied.

"You know we gonna hold it down," she assured.

"Thanks baby-girl," he managed to say before he pushed the end button.

Vito had jumped on the phone with Larissa by the time he had hung the phone up with Deidra so he decided to call Firebug and feed him the bad news.

"Your time to speak," Firebug answered the phone.

"What up pop?"

"What up youngun?"

"A lot of drama, they just snatched up Slanga."

"Say it ain't so," he whined out.

"I wish I could, but I just got the news myself."

"Well, do you want me to cancel the twins trip?" He asked.

"Na'll, I was just calling to see when they were leaving. You know shit don't stop. It's hard for a broke man to overcome this, so the grind must go on."

"True that," Firebug replied, "I'll have them rolling out of here around seven, so you know what time you should be expecting them."

"I'll be waiting. Just tell him to hit me up if something looks shiesty."

"How is Manda holding up?" Firebug asked with concern.

"I really can't call it, but hit her up and see for yourself."

"I think I'll do that, but when you coming to see me?"

"I ain't in a position to be moving right now."

"We always in a position to move youngun, and never forget that. Never get so stuck in your own shit or the shit around you."

"True, and be safe out there Pop."

"You do the same and make sure you take care of my girls."

"Don't I always," Kruger replied before hanging up.

Vito had already broken his conversation with Larissa so when he saw his cousin take the phone from his ear he asked, "You alright?"

"Yeah, just some more shit a playa has to deal with."

"I can feel you on that. On our way to Atlanta you get a call from your partner in prison, but on the way back you get another call about your other partner getting locked-up."

"It's just another chapter," Kruger replied with a sly grin.

Vito just smiled, "Sometimes it feels as if, nothing good is ever going to happen for a nigga."

Kruger looked over at his cousin and stressed, "Man, everything happens for a reason, we just have to peep game. If that third eye closed you'll never decipher day from night."

They both rode in silence for the remaining of the ride. Neither of the two spoke another word until they pulled in the driveway.

"You done came along way on a mental aspect," Vito stressed as he stepped out of the truck.

"I feel the same way about you," Kruger responded as they walked towards his front door.

"Just know that if you need me, I'm here."

Kruger looked over at him with a sly grin, "What's understood doesn't need to be talked about!"

****

Baby Gotti was sitting at the dinning table while Lil Dusty was on the phone with Fredel. He watched how Lil Dusty's facial expression changed from a smile to a frown during the conversation.

"What's up fool?" Babby Gotti questioned the moment the call was over.

"They locked Slanga up earlier today," he replied with a look of disappointment.

"You bullshitting?!" He responded with a similar expression.

"I wish I was," he replied in a mournful manner, "but Fredel said by the time we ready to cope again he gonna try to put us down with Slanga homeboy, some cat name Kruger."

"I don't know dude, but I done heard his name before," he stated as he started to roll a blunt.

"Cuz say that they working with the same shit though, and nine times out of ten he'll let it go for the same price."

"Whatever, just as long as this fool ain't DEA."

"I seriously doubt that cuz would turn us on to a undercover.:"

"In this shit how can you doubt anything bra?" Baby Gotti stressed as he lit up a blunt.

"So what time are you going to pick up the girls?" Lil Dusty asked him.

"Man, you going too, cause I ain't riding all the way down there by myself," he responded as he raised from his chair and walked in the kitchen.

"Bra, I ain't going nowhere. You shouldn't have told them that you was coming to get them. I've told you're in love ass about that bullshit! You can't keep your eyes on Michelle and your money at the same time."

"Fuck you nigga!" Baby Gotti retorted as he walked back in with a fifth of *Crown Royal* in one hand and the blunt in the other, "I don't say shit when you be all up Tiffany's ass!"

After sitting down and taking a few pulls of the blunt, he passed it and asked, "So, you saying that I shouldn't go get them?"

Lil Dusty took a pull from the blunt before pausing for a moment and answering, "All I'm saying is M.O.B., you do the math."

-KRUGER-

At times like this a playa has no time for self. Now picture waking up to five different females who's been wilding all night. The only perk was breakfast in bed. At least that's the part Vito claimed he liked the most.

Stacy and Tracy rolled through around 9:30, so I couldn't just let them get on the road that time of night. Besides, I knew Amanda could really use the company.

As soon as those crazy twins walked in, all hell broke loose. They ended up having a little slumber party in the living room, and I ended up waking up next to Vito in my bed. To top it all off, me and this fool sleeping in a room full of money, bricks of coke and dogg food, plus a few pounds of purple. Being spook isn't even a question.

I talked to Hammah earlier and he tripped when he heard all them females in the background. Naturally, he was crushed when I told him about Slanga, but he know just like I know, that's just how shit be. I asked him about Bad-Azz and he said that everything is everything with him too. It's funny how you never recognize the love you have for your peoples until they're gone.

As I look at the position I'm holding out here, I can't help but smile. I know my foundation ain't concrete, but a playa ain't starving either. When I look at Hammah and Bad-Azz, and all of the other hustlers behind them walls and fences, I have to ask myself, is all this shit even worth it?

I remember something that the preacher asked me and Vito the other day. The question was, are we happy with the way we living? And you know he ain't allow us to answer right then. He just wanted us to think on it for a few days. You know with me being me, I wanted to ask him the same question, even though I know he was gonna say yeah, but then he could've surprised me. I know he a preacher and all, but buddy breath like I breath, so I know he's cursed with regrets too.

When I think about it, I really don't have a choice but to be happy with it. To many people depending on me out here. It may sound crazy to others, but it is what it is with me.

Here I am waiting on Burger to scoop me up. Vito dipped out with the girls to go shopping about a half an hour ago. I should've told Deidra to take this package to the spot, but I'll call and remind her later. I would take it myself, but I'll be with Burger. It ain't that I don't trust him, but only a fool will open that door of opportunity.

That gotta be this fool ringing the doorbell like he done lost his mind.

"What's up playboy?" I stated with a sly grin after I opened the door.

"Shit, where the weed at?" He asked as if he was a true fiend.

"Man, you gotta slow down on that shit if it got you like that," I chuckled out as he walked to the dining table.

"Dam!" He stressed after seeing the pound of purple I had on the table, "Either you're one of the boldest or one of the stupidest cats in the world, either way it ain't good."

"Man, I'm just being me," I replied as I threw him a box of blunts.

"You got straight yet?" He asked as he pulled one of the blunts out of the box.

"What makes you think that I wasn't before?"

"I just know you was trying to let Slanga do his thing."

"True, but what you wanted?" I asked as I walked to the kitchen and grabbed the half of gallon of orange juice.

"I need like one and a half this time, I have a few cats from across the water coming through."

"Well, I gotta get it to you a little later, cause ole girl them out there shopping and shit, but you know I definitely got you," I replied as I grabbed my keys and headed towards the door.

"Dam fool, you just gonna leave this loud ass weed on the table like this?" He interjected after rolling a blunt.

I looked over at him and then at the table and realized how right he was. I gotta be losing my mind to just walk out and leave this out like that. I walked in the kitchen and grabbed one of those kitchen trash bags and raked it all in, before taking it in the back with the rest of the federal case I had in the house. I definitely had to call Deidra, asap.

✱✱✱✱✱✱✱✱✱✱✱✱✱✱

"What's up nephew?" The fat guy behind the counter greeted Red as he stepped inside the *Spur* gas station.

"What up unk?" Red replied as he walked to the back of the store and grabbed a beer.

"They tell me that you're around the corner knocking muthafuckas out!" The fat guy stated with great interest.

"Unk, you should know better than to listen to that shit you hear in the hood," Red replied as he walked back to the counter.

"You know that I gotta keep an ear to the streets for shit like that when it comes down to ya'll," he stated in a concerned manner, "I owe that much to Bad-Azz."

"And Bad-Azz know, just like you know, that we gonna handle ours!" Red replied in an agitated manner before adding, "When have you known us to need an overseer?"

"You know that I ain't trying to be that," he responded in his defense, "and I don't think that I'm about to let you pay for that beer."

Red looked at the fat guy with a devilish grin before stressing, "Look unk, it ain't no animosity between me and you or nothing, but I really just think you need to mind your own. And as far as this little brew," he added as he dug in his pocket, "I can take care of that."

"You shouldn't act like that nephew," he implied while pushing the two dollars back towards Red.

"I was just standing here thinking the same thing about you," Red responded with the same smirk as he walked out of the store leaving the money on the counter.

As soon as Red walked out of the store he was surrounded by two detective cars.

"Mr. Cabbage, can you please place your hands on the hood?" One of the smaller detectives stated after he jumped out of the first vehicles.

"What in the hell have I done now?" Red asked in a calm manner as he opened his beer.

"We'll talk about that down at the station," the passenger of the second car answered.

"Well, at least let me get a sip of this brew I just bought before ya'll go snatching me up," he responded before turning the 22 ounce bottle up and downing half of it.

The detectives just looked at each other as if they couldn't believe his actions.

"Do ya'll mind if I finish this. I promise I'll kill it on this one," Red assured with a smile exposing his eight gold fronts.

There were a few minor hustlers in front of the gas station who started cheering Red on. This obviously pissed the detectives off because as soon as Red turned the bottle up, they rushed him.

After they had him in handcuffs Red stressed, "Now, if I was gonna run or something, I probably would've deserved this harassment, but ya'll already know what time it is with me."

"You should've ran muthafucka, so I could've bust your ass!" The passenger of the first car retorted.

"Run from you, for what?!" Red disgustedly stressed, "You ain't nobody that I should be afraid of. Now, If I was to step to you, would you run from me?! I don't think so! So why should I run from your soft ass, you're a coward hiding behind a badge! People like me don't run from people like you!" He managed to add before they stuffed him the backseat and speeded away.

****

"Do you think that Kruger gonna look out for Lil Dusty them like Slanga did?" Fredel was asking Kay-Kay as they sat in Gunslanga's trap watching television and smoking a blunt.

"Yeah, he gonna look out. If you think Kruger gonna let some money get by him, you got it twisted," she responded with smoke seeping from her nose and mouth.

"I think I might go out there with Lil Dusty them for a few," Fredel revealed.

"I thought you didn't want to mess with family like that?" She questioned.

"Hell, when you look at it, that's all that I'm doing with you right here," he replied as he grabbed the blunt she was passing.

"Well, do what you feel, but I'm good where I'm at."

"Yeah, I think that's what I'm gonna do," he said in a tone as if he was convincing himself.

"So, when do you plan on making that move?" She asked as she raised from the couch and headed towards the kitchen.

"Probably later on tonight or tomorrow."

"You owe Slanga something?" She asked from the kitchen.

"Yeah, like three stacks."

"Well, you need to stay here until you give Kruger that money, or at least holler at him about it," she suggested as she walked back in the living room with a cup of ice.

"For what?" He asked with a look of confusion.

"Nigga, you better open your eyes and recognize what's going on and who you fucking with!"

"I know who I'm fucking with!" He retorted, "Me and Kruger was locked up together."

"I can't tell!" She stressed as she rolled her eyes at him, "If you knew who you was fucking with you wouldn't be asking me for what. Now, one thing I've learned about these crazy ass niggas is they don't play the radio about that check. True enough you and Slanga cool, but when you don't attempt to pay him his money, he's gonna put that cool shit to the side."

Fredel watched as she poured her a cup of cognac before he stressed, "I never said that I

258

wasn't gonna pay him. I just said that I wanted to relocate for a few."

"Now put yourself in Slanga shoes. How would you feel about a nigga relocating who still owe me."

"I ain't look at it like that," he confessed.

She just shook her head with a sly grin before replying, "Well cuz, I can guarantee that is just how they gonna be looking at it."

(CHAPTER 7)

"So Mr. Ford," Detective McNeil was saying to Weasel, "what am I gonna do with you?"

They sat across from each other in the interrogation room A on the second floor of 401 Walton Way.

"Pretty much the same thing you've been doing with me," Weasel replied with a sly grin, "ask me where I was around a certain time and date, and eventually let me go."

The detective was openly agitated as he took a deep breath, "I'm gonna be honest with you Weasel, I really don't dig Mondays too funny. And being in here with you this early in the morning isn't helping at all."

"Look playboy, I don't wanna be here just as much as you claim you don't want me here," he replied with an sincere expression, "but let's remember who came and got who."

Detective McNeil nodded his head as he sat back in his chair and stressed, "The only reason that you're sitting in front of me is that your car was seen in the victim's parking lot the same night the murders occurred. Now just tell me this, how come your name pops up in at least forty percent of the cases I get?"

"Well, from the outside looking in, one would think that I'm being harassed."

"And from the inside looking out?" The detective quizzically questioned.

"I would hope that you'll say the same," he replied with a phony smile.

The detective lightly chuckled at the comment before saying, "Well, from my point of view I would say that I'm just doing my job. So if you don't mind, could you explain to me what went on that night."

"I really don't have to explain nothing to you. I could easily call my lawyer to come and explain it for me," Weasel replied with a sinister grin before adding, "but with me and you being so accustomed to this here, I'll tell you like this. The reason my car was in that parking lot was, it shut down on me. Now, I have a tow truck receipt and a copy of the mechanics diagnostics, if you wanna see them."

The detective just shook his head before he stressed, "We all know what you're doing out there. Do you actually think your untouchable?" He asked in a fatherly tone. "Now, I've watched you grow up with my daughter, and to be honest with you, I'd hate to see you get the chair. So from me to you, I advise that you slow down before you find yourself in a sticky situation. But Weasel, if I find out that you had anything to do with any case that's made it to my desk, you might as well get ready for that chair."

"Can I go now?"

"You could've left five minutes ago."

"Have a nice day Mr. McNeil," he stated as he raised from the chair.

"Do you need a ride home?" The detective asked with a phony smile.

"Na'll playboy, I can walk. You know I don't ride with Babylon's servants, unless I have no other choice."

****

"Man, I can't wait until we find buddy that got Red locked up," Rip stated as he sat on the porch of 1122 along with Hamburger, Georgia Slim and Kruger.

"I wish you could've seen the fool screaming he a OG and all. Now come to find out he done pressed charges on a playa," Pimp stated openly disgusted.

"Red said they was looking for you too," Kruger stressed, "but he told them that ain't nobody else hit him."

"I see that I can't go nowhere for the weekend and come back and expect everything to be all good," Georgia Slim stressed.

"So much shit happens in an hour," Hamburger inquired, "so you can imagine what happens in a weekend."

"The best thing that happen was we got to talk to Hammah!" Rip stressed, "Now that fool is living it up with the cell-phone and all in prison."

"Nigga, you know we gonna do our thing no matter where they send us," Pimp stressed with a wide grin, "I'm trying to take the devil customers if I go to hell."

"Dummy there ain't no Gee's in hell!" Red stressed with authority, "Gangsta's make the world go round."

Pimp nodded his head in agreement as all the other fellas burst out laughing.

"Man that looks like Weasel walking up the sidewalk," Rip stressed.

"That's him," Hamburger confirmed.

Pimp was the first to open his mouth when Weasel got within ear shot, "Dam Weasel, what a baller like you doing walking?"

Weasel just smirked at the sarcastic question, "You know them people love fucking with a playa about something."

"What they fucking with you about now?" Rip asked breaking the brief silence.

"Some dead people, but it ain't nothing," Weasel replied as he took a seat on the porch.

"Who fucking with you?" Kruger asked.

"Your father in law," Weasel revealed with a sly grin before he added, "you know he been trying to get me since the first grade."

All the fellas burst out laughing but Big Ox who just asked, "You actually think it's been that long?"

No-one paid him any attention as Kruger rose from his seat and stressed, "Bra, you know you have to keep a straight face with that cat."

"Where you about to go?" Hamburger asked.

"I have to check on Slanga trap," Kruger replied before jumping off the porch.

"Dam nigga," Weasel stressed, "I was hoping that I could catch a ride from you."

"I can take you cuz," Pimp implied before adding, "I was about to head out for a minute anyway."

"There you go right there," Kruger stated with a sly grin before heading down the sidewalk towards Gunslanga's trap.

As he walked down the street his phone rang.

"Yeah, what's up?" He stated after seeing that it was Teresa.

"Hey baby," she stated in an excited manner, "do you think I'm gonna be able to steal some time with you today?"

"Of course you can. I'm in the middle of something right now, but I can meet up with you a little later."

"What time are we talking about?"

"Anytime after three."

"That's cool, cause I have a few things that I have to take care of myself."

"You need anything?"

"I'm alright for now, but I'm definitely gonna need a little something- something when I see you," she responded in a seductive manner that had him smiling from ear to ear.

"Oh yeah?" He questioned with a huge grin on his face.

"Of course," she replied, "you know it's time to feed the baby."

"Well, let me finish this in front of me and I got you.."

"Alright boo, I'll see you in a little while."

"Make sure you get plenty of rest," he replied before he hung up.

When he finally reached Gunslanga's trap, he realized that the porch was abandoned. When he walked in the house the first thing he noticed was Vader knocked out on the couch. He just stood over him for a minute and shook his head before he walked in Kay-Kay's room. Just as he thought, she too was stretched out on the bed fast asleep.

"Kay-Kay," he called out as he slapped her on the ass.

"Dam, can a bitch sleep in this muthafucka!" She practically screamed out without realizing who had woke her.

"Girl, if you don't get your ass up!" Kruger stressed as he slapped her on the ass again.

She immediately jumped up and apologized.

"What the hell you got the door wide open for and you back here sleep?!" He questioned.

Kay-Kay's face had a swirl designs imprinted in it from the cheap blanket she was laying on.

"You need to get up and wash your face," he stated with a chuckle before he walked out her room and straight towards Vader.

"Vader!" He stated as he shook him awoke.

After recognizing who had woke him he stated, "I know that I have a nice wake up coming, at least a ball."

"Nigga, you lucky that I ain't putting my foot in your ass!" He retorted, "Why you got this door wide open and you in here sleep like you done got somebody pregnant?!"

"That door was open?" He rebutted, "I made sure I closed it before I laid down."

"You might have made sure it was closed but your dumb ass ain't make sure it was locked."

"Fredel told me to leave the door open for him," he responded in a pleading manner.

"Where he at?"

"He went to get something to eat early this morning," he whined out.

"Fool, you've been trapping around here all your life, but you gonna listen to a nigga who been trapping around here for a few weeks?!"

Kruger snapped as he slapped Vader across the head.

"I,I,I,I thought," he started to stutter out before Kruger cut him off.

"That's your problem right there!" He stated with aggression, "See you had no business thinking! You're the eyes, not the brain. The eyes does only what the brain tells them too."

"My bad Kruger, did something get missing?" Vader asked openly disappointed in himself.

"Na'll, but that ain't the point," he confessed.

"So everything straight?" Vader questioned with a little more confidence.

"Yeah, everything good," Kruger replied.

"You mean to tell me that ain't nobody came in here and stole nothing and you making all this fuss! Muthafucka, you owe me a major break off now!"

Kruger couldn't help but burst out laughing before replying with, "I don't have nothing on me right now, but I'll make sure I get you something before I dip."

"Where you about to go?" Vader asked as Kruger walked towards the bathroom.

Kruger paid him no mind as he asked Kay-Kay what she wanted to spend.

"Six," she replied with a frown before adding, "and I need some dick."

Kruger just shook his head before looking at Vader who just shrugged his shoulders. Kruger said nothing more as he walked out the door.

****

Jimmy and Surina sat on the couch inside their suite off of Stevens Creek Road, watching television. There was very unfamiliar vibe in the room. In their hearts, they both knew that the relationship they once had was far gone, but they held on to the familiarity.

"Can you tell me why you're sitting here just staring into space?" Jimmy questioned after noticing she wasn't watching the show she practically begged him to watch.

"I'm sorry baby, I just have a lot on my mind right now," was her only response.

"Maybe if you wasn't so quick to answer my phone you wouldn't have that much to think about," Jimmy interjected before raising from the couch and grabbing the brown duffle bag.

After seeing him grab the bag she asked, "Where you going now?"

"I got a few things I need to tend to," he replied as he headed towards the door.

"But you just got back," she whined out.

"Look Surina," he stressed as he turned around to face her, "I have things to take care of that require my full attention. And since we both have other things on our minds, I would rather be giving my time to them."

She watched as he walked out the door and couldn't help but shake her head. She knew that it was all her fault, if only she didn't answer his phone. How was she suppose to know that it was Deamon who was calling.

The trust issues between her and Jimmy was already at an all time high considering the time she was spending with her military friend. Never in a million years would she believe that her relationship with Jimmy would end up being nothing more than sex.

After she gave Jimmy the phone, he didn't talk to Deamon long at all and that bothered her. Rather she wanted to admit it or not Deamon and Jimmy corresponding on any level had her mind boggling. The moment they were off the phone Jimmy put on his clothes and walked out of the room with a black duffle bag.

She didn't want to add fuel, to the already lit flame, by asking where he was going, so she just let him walk out without uttering a word.

He was gone for almost an hour before he returned with a brown duffle bag that he ended up sitting by the television. It almost tore her to pieces wondering what was in that bag. The contents in that bag is what was on her mind when Jimmy walked out on her.

She sat there and thought of all the reason these two would collaborate. She even considered the fact that Kruger had something to do with Tom-Tom's murder. In her mind Jimmy just didn't have the heart while Weasel never possessed the brain. She knew that Kruger possessed both attributes, and from her personal experiences with him, she also knew when it came down to his money, he was far past unpredictable.

-KRUGER-

Amanda left with the twins this morning headed back to the C-Port like an hour after Vito and his wifey dipped. I guess Slanga told her to go and free her mind for a minute, cause I know she wouldn't have just left without him knowing.

Deidra was suppose to go to work today, but she called in, again. I don't know what kind of hold she has on her manager, but buddy be letting her off whenever she wants to be. Right now she's gone to take care of something for me.

I talked to Luther this morning and he thanked me for getting that dogg food back, he even gave me a few ounces. Now I don't know where to begin when it comes down to getting rid of this shit, but I'm sure Firebug can assist me in some way.

Luther screaming that he want me to hold down a position on his team, but you know I had to turn him down, at least for now anyway. As odd as it may sound, I don't murder for money, it's always the principle. The only reason I rode with cuz-o was curiosity. Believe me, when I go to that extreme, my target has seriously violated.

273

Another reason I declined was in my family it ain't no such thing as one man above the crew, we deal in EQUALITY. If we have a problem, we call a family meeting and don't just no one muthafucka do the talking. Now tell me how I can give all that up to answer to some other cat? Luther is a cool dude, and I do respect who and what he is, but honestly, I'll be a fool to leave a family I've helped establish.

Here it is almost two o'clock and I'm suppose to meet with Teresa in a few. The only reason I'm trying to give her sometime is she'd been looking out for Hammah. Well, I lie, because she could still get it regardless. I hope this ain't her calling me now though.

"Yeah what's up?" I stated after answering.

"What up bra?"

"Who this, Hammah?"

"Playboy, what I told you about asking and answering questions in the same sentence," I heard my comrade stress.

"What up bra?"

"Shit, just chillen, high as a muthafucka."

"That's love in itself."

"Show you right."

"You need anything."

"Na'll bra, that little bit you sent through got a playa sitting lovely."

"So when do you think they gonna ship you back out?"

"It ain't no telling, they still screaming the x-ray machine is down. So they really got a nigga on standby to see if they can fix something I already know is broken."

"Man, you know how the state do, but at least you can bid a little better with the accessories."

"Yeah, you right, by the way tell Tamika that some nigga name Keenan called her."

"My nigga, I didn't tell you that she pregnant, I think he the baby daddy."

"You bullshitting!"

"I wish I was playboy, but it is what it is."

"How the nigga look? I mean how he act?"

"My folk, believe it or not, I haven't even met the cat yet."

"Nigga, you know you tripping! You gotta grab that cat and man handle him. Maybe tie him up and beat with a hot hanger or some shit like that, just to let him know what to expect if he violates."

"Yeah, that sounds tempting, but you know she's already hot at me about her phone I sent you."

"Tell her, dam this phone," he chuckled out, "But word is that you and Slanga really good."

"Some what, but everybody sitting alright out here on the Summer."

"If everybody getting money like that, it's time to switch shit up."

Now this fool telling me the same shit everybody else been screaming. What is this, some type of sign from the higher power?

"That's respect," is all I could reply with.

"The real live by the codes, but the genuine are the codes," I heard him say, "now, it's on you to chose which one you are."

"Dam nigga, you already know who I be."

"That's what's up, just make sure you spread the gospel then. But I gotta jet off this horn before these Babylonians come through."

"Holla if you need something."

"You already know bra, much love though."

"Til death!" I stated before pushing the end button.

I miss my homie more than anything these days. He's one of the reasons I'm out here grinding so hard. What I look like not having him something out here when he step out. Hell, he helped build this Summer Street shit from the dirt.

-TERESA-

"What the fuck you mean Ron found out?!" I found myself blasting on Toya's grimy ass over the phone.

"I don't know how he found out, but he did," she nonchalantly replied as if the situation wasn't serious at all.

"So what did Ron say, I mean did he trip?" I just had to know.

"Yeah and no," she replied before pausing and adding, "at first he did, but then I let him know why we went and he really couldn't help but respect it."

"You're lucky that he didn't knock your ass out!" I retorted.

She just giggled at the comment before she reminded me, "You know that I can handle Ron. The only reason that I'm telling you about it is, I don't know if he's gonna tell Deamon."

"That's exactly what I'm sitting here thinking about," I heard myself whisper through the receiver, "But how do you think he found out?"

"It really don't matter how he found out, the question is, what are you going to do about it?"

"Maybe I need to tell him before someone else does. I really don't think that he'll be mad about it though, being that he gave me money to send him. Besides, he knows that I don't want nothing to do with David."

"Teresa," she said my name as if she was tired of talking to me, "You already know how big Deamon is about things like this, so don't expect him to take the news kindly. True, he approved of you looking out for David, if that's what you wanted to do, but with you doing it behind his back, that's a whole different situation."

Now I know this isn't the same bitch that begged me to sneak off with her. That's why I really didn't want to deal with her on that level. It's like every time we get involve with men, her respect for our friendship diminishes.

"You know I wouldn't even went if it wasn't for your ass!" I still found myself blasting.

"Both of us know that, but to him it looks as if you went for your own personal reasons, since you waited so long to tell him."

She just keeps coming with it, "So what do you suggest I do?" I asked in a sarcastic manner.

"I really can't call that one," she replied before adding, "he's your man, you should know how to handle your man."

"You're right Toya, I got it from here," I stated openly disgusted.

"If it's worth anything, I'm sorry that I drag you in the middle of this."

Now I see what Deamon was talking about when he said something about that sorry shit, because she's right. She is definitely a sorry excuse for a friend.

"Don't worry about it," I stated before adding, "but let me prepare for my nightmare."

"Alright girl, good luck."

"Yeah," is all I responded with as I hung the phone up.

"Yeah, thanks for nothing," I found myself saying as I laid on the bed and stared at the ceiling.

When is this unnecessary drama gonna cease in my life? Can someone please give me the answer to that!

Now this nigga gonna think that I did those things for Hammah because I was in the wrong for some other shit. I wish I would've seen this going down, maybe I would've told him before I went. I know he would've let me go with no problem. Now with the help of this bitch, it looks as if I'm keeping secrets.

I have to be the dumbest bitch alive to allow a muthafucka who consistently shows me that she's my primary enemy, come and encourage me to make a stupid move like that.

Hell, knowing Deamon, he already know! The nigga just waiting to see if or when I'm gonna tell him. That's just how his ass is. With that being said, I have no choice but to tell him. Now I just have to come up with a good way to do it.

****

Baby Gotti opened the door for an angry Lil Dusty, who had apparently been ranging the doorbell for the last five minutes. Under normal circumstances he wouldn't have to sweat it, but he knew that the only reason it took Baby Gotti so long to answer the door was the fact that he was laying up with Michelle.

"Every time I come over here you're laying up with this broad, playing house and shit!" Lil Dusty snapped.

Baby Gotti gave him a sly smirk before he replied, "I'm one of the few who can do that and get money."

"Now tell me this," Lil Dusty implied as he took a seat on the couch, "how are we gonna get this mil-ticket if you keep thinking with your dick?"

"See what you fail to realize is that I'm ready to ree-up, what about you?"

Lil Dusty couldn't help but smirk before stressing, "What you think I'm over here for?"

"Well, we need to get Fredel to holler at that cat Kruger and we can go from there."

"I have enough to get two on my own, what you working with?" Lil Dusty asked.

"Now tell me how I look letting you get two and I'm still at one, this Baby Gotti nigga!" He retorted with a wide grin.

"Well, I guess we'll be doubling up on this one," he replied as he pulled out his phone.

"And you thought that I was slipping on my pimping," Baby Gotti stressed as he walked towards the bedroom before adding, "picture that shit!"

-KRUGER-

I just got off the phone with Firebug and he wants me to go to Vegas with him in a few weeks, but I don't know if I'll be able to make that trip. Too much going on around me. What would that really say about me if I was to haul ass like that? But I do have to do go check on his ass, cause I've really been slipping on that.

Deidra at the house cleaning up. I told her that I should be home a little late tonight. The way she's been running around, she'll be sleep by the time I get there anyway. I have to make sure I do something special for her this week, just to let her know how much I really appreciate her being who she is to me. Because there's no way I could accomplish all that I do, without her.

Without all that said, that's probably why I always feel as if I'm committing a carnal sin when I'm about to spend time with Teresa. For some strange reason I feel I'm stabbing Deidra in the back or some shit like that, being that she's the one I'm really connected to. Maybe Deidra is the one. Maybe I just need to stop playing games with myself and just look at things in the right perspective. But every time I try to look at it like that, I realize that I can't leave Teresa either. At least not as long as she's carrying my seed.

I'm surprised that she ain't hit me up complaining about how late I am. I have to admit though, she's really started to act alot better. But the fact still remains that she could never be what Deidra is to me, and for that reason alone, her pink slip is past due.

Weasel got at me the other day and let me know about the Phylisha incident. I guess I'm that one person that he feels he can confide in. Little he know, he was my biggest inspiration when I stepped out. I mean to see your homie coping byrds, I mean this the little gangsta you fed the game to. He showed me that anything's possible out here.

I just told him to keep his nose clean and stay away from them trifling ass bitches and those so called homies that hate to see a playa doing good. He should be straight though, all he has to do is stay focus.

As far as that cat Jimmy is concerned, the day he gets rid of Surina is the day he'll be more level headed. I just served that nigga six bricks for 23 apiece. Weasel told me that he don't trust him too funny, but I'm like if you don't trust him, why did you bring him in the mist of my cipher. He has to know that regardless of Jimmy's actions, he's responsible.

Now this can't be nobody but Teresa....

"I'm pulling up now," I stressed after answering.

"Say Kruger, this Fredel," I hear ole boy say.

"My bad playboy, I thought you was somebody else," I replied after pulling in the apartment building.

"Na'll, my folk, just me."

"True, what up though."

"Did you get that from Kay-Kay?"

"Yeah, I picked that up earlier," I replied as I stepped out of the truck and headed to the apartment.

"Cool, but I needed to holler at you."

Me and bra ain't never did no business, so naturally I'm kind of weary, but I still had to see what he talking about, "Where you at?"

"Woodlake off of Windsor Springs."

"How long you gonna be there?"

"I should be here for a minute."

"Well, call me back in ten minutes, I should be out that way so you can give me directions," I stated as I walked in the apartment and stood by the door.

Tamika is at her usual spot with them books in front of her. It brought a smile to my face knowing that she wants something more out life than what she sees on a daily. I think that every hustler needs to see that every now and then. It builds inspiration.

"Alright playboy, ten minutes," I heard Fredel stress in an impatient manner.

I didn't even say shit, I just hung the phone up. Me and this cat was locked up together one time, but we never talked on that level. The next thing I know he's grinding with Slanga.

The moment Tamika saw me take the phone from my ear she stresses, "You know that girl ain't ready yet."

Now this the first time I've seen her act like this when she spoke of Teresa, so I know off top that something has went down between them.

"I need you to take me to Woodlake," I said as I walked to the bedroom.

When I stepped in the room, I went straight to the bottom drawer of my dresser and grabbed one of the twins, and slid it in the seams of my jeans. I had a t-shirt on so it was nothing to conceal it. I just hope that I don't have to use this muthafucka!

When I walked to the bathroom door, I could hear the shower running, so I knew that I still had a minute before she got right.

"Say Teresa," I stated as I opened the door and allowed the steam to hit me in the face.

"I'll be out in a second boo," she yelled back.

She really sounded as if she was trying to catch a nut in the shower.

"Just save me some," I managed to chuckle out before I added, "I'm about to take Tamika to the store right fast."

"Alright boo, just hurry back."

"I gotcha," I replied before closing the door and walking towards the front door.

Twenty minutes later me and sis were pulling in their driveway.

"Sit here until I get back," I told her as I stepped out, "but don't turn the truck off," I added before closing the door and walking towards the front door where Fredel greeted me.

"What up playboy, what you had on your mind?" I asked as he lead me in the house.

"My cousin and his partner trying to get some work," he replied as I followed him into what had to be the living room, where two young cats sat on the couch, "Kruger, this my cousin Lil Dusty and his people Baby Gotti."

I wasn't feeling this get comfortable shit so I induced the conversation, "So what's the word?"

"Well my folk," the one he introduced as Lil Dusty stated, "it's just like cuz said, we trying to get some work, and since Slanga locked up, Fredel trying to turn us on to you."

"What ya'll looking for?"

"At least four," he replied with.

"What did Slanga let ya'll get it for?"

"We ain't buy nothing but two the last time, but he taxed us twenty-eight a piece."

"Well, I don't know if I can let ya'll get it for that right now, I'll have to make a few phone calls," I stated as I took my eyes away from Lil Dusty and looked over at the too quiet Baby Gotti, "but I'll call ya'll in thirty minutes and let ya'll know something."

"That's what's up," Lil Dusty replied as he raised from his spot on the couch and walked Kruger towards the front door, "we appreciate you coming by, even if you don't come through for us."

I couldn't help but smile at this cat, "Playboy, that ain't nothing, I just hope that I can help you."

****

Kay-Kay sat on the couch with Big Ox watching the movie *The Untouchables* when her phone rang.

"What's good," she stated after answering.

"What up Ms. So-Anxious?"

"What up sexy?" She replied with a wide grin after realizing it was Kruger.

"You," he answered, "I need some information from you."

"Anything for you."

"Who are Lil Dusty and Baby Gotti?"

"Lil Dusty my little cousin and Baby Gotti his partner, that's who Fredel went to hustle with."

"Has Slanga ever served them?"

"Yeah, he served them last week. I know they bought two, but I don't know how much he charged them."

"Preciate that," he stated before asking, "who there with you?"

"You know Vader on the porch and Ox is right here," she replied as she looked over at Ox.

"Let me holler at that fool," he stated.

"What up bra?" Big Ox asked with his eyes still glued to the television.

"Just trying to make sure ya'll straight."

"I'm good for now, but I might holler at you in the morning the way shit popping down here."

"I feel that," Kruger replied with a chuckle, "It's totally different rotating with two muthafuckas instead of seven or eight, huh?"

"You got that shit right!" Big Ox agreed.

"Just call me in the morning."

"Say no more bra and much love!"

"Til death big homie."

(CHAPTER 8)

-TERESA-

I don't know how Deamon really took what I told him last night. Well, I know it hurt him in some way or the other, because when I tried to get in the shower with him he told me that he needed to take it alone.

When he finally came out of the bathroom, he put on his clothes without saying a word. When I asked him was he mad at me, the nigga just looked at me and shook his head, "Mad at you for what? I can't get mad at you, if anything babygirl, I'm mad at myself."

It's not that he said it in a harsh manner or anything, but I know he was only being sarcastic. I tried to tell him that I was sorry, but as soon as I got sorry out, he gave me that satisfied look that said, "I already know." I knew right then that I had just played the hell out of myself.

On his way out the door I wanted to say something, anything, to make him understand, but all I could conjure up with was, "Deamon, you know I love you?"

He just gave me that crazy look again and walked over to the bed and gave me a peck on the lips, "I don't know why you tripping, like I told you, if anything I'm mad at myself."

I couldn't even sleep last night because I don't know how he's walking around really thinking. Now here I am with the day off and nothing to do, but I already know that he ain't even thinking about spending time with me.

It seems that when it comes down to our relationship, I can't do anything right. It's always the small stuff that I find myself fucking up on. I mean, all I had to do was tell him I wanted to go see David from the jump and I wouldn't even be going through this.

When I put myself in his shoes, I can see why he would trip, but hell, at least I'm the one that told his ass. It's not like I went to a hotel room with David or something.

What really made me realize how disappointed he was in me is when I tried to tell him what we were talking about. He waved me off and stressed, "That's really none of my business what ya'll talked about."

STILL STUCK

After I studied his face for a moment I finally realized that he didn't look crazy, mad or anything out of the ordinary. It was the tone of his voice that had me feeling so disappointed in myself. He acted as if I hadn't said anything, he was emotionless. That's when that old question came to mind again, "Are we really meant to be together?"

I mean, can I really handle the responsibilities of being Mrs. Pearsey? But then there are those times when I can't believe that I asked myself a dumb ass question like that.

Toya said just give him a few days and everything should pan out, but listening to her ass is what got me in this fucked up position in the first place. She wants me to pick her up from work so she can buy me lunch. If it wasn't for me wanting to get out of this house, I wouldn't go nowhere with her shady ass.

✶✶✶✶✶✶✶✶✶✶✶✶✶✶

"Dam playboy," Baby Gotti was saying to Fredel who was sitting on the couch watching television, "you been up all night?"

"Hell yeah, that's where the money at," Fredel answered with a wide grin.

"So how much did you go through?" He asked as he took a seat next to him with a blunt dangling from his mouth.

"Well, you know we only whipped up a half last night," he stated as he flicked his lighter and allowed Baby Gotti to light the blunt before adding, "well, I only have two ounces of that left."

"Now that's straight for a Monday night," he replied as cloud of smoke raised over his head.

"Hell yeah, that's straight for out here!" Fredel excitedly agreed.

"Nigga what, you thought we wasn't getting money out here or something?" Baby Gotti sarcastically replied, "See this out here is where all the army cats come to get straight, and you know how they like to stay high."

"I can feel that, but that ain't all that come through," he replied, "I served my old chemistry teacher last night, now that really tripped me out."

"Well, you'll be tripping all day on the muthafuckas who come through here. From teachers, preachers, to circuit court judges, they all come to spend money with a playa."

"Hell, I was thinking with all the traffic coming through, we might need to get a runner outside. It's best to send them to the back instead of letting all them muthafuckers knock on the front door. Cause with people knowing that I'm gonna be up all night, it's really gonna crank up."

"That cool, but it's gonna be hard to find somebody who gonna ride all night," he replied as he passed Fredel the blunt.

"You got one right down the street, the cat ya'll call Batman. Hell, he rolled through and helped me a little last night."

"That nigga owe me three hundred!"

"My folk, I'll pay that tab out of my pocket," Fredel insisted, "the way I see it, I'll make way more than that little change. Besides, the nigga know everybody out here. That means he knows who and who not to serve."

"I can feel you on that."

"Man, you should've coped some of that dro from Kruger too," Fredel stressed after looking down at the blunt in disgust, "he working with that A-1 shit."

"He seems as if he's gonna be alright," Baby Gotti implied with a cool smile.

"I been locked up with bra and he good peoples. I mean if he eating, we eating, that's just how he is. But Kay-Kay the one always giving him the purple ribbon though."

Baby Gotti just burst out laughing before stressing, "That just means that he's serving her the wood!"

****

Kruger and Deidra sat at the window booth inside *Applebee's*. Deidra wore a loose fitting navy blue business suit that concealed her pregnancy under a soft pink blouse. Kruger couldn't help but gaze at her from time to time.

He could see the effects the baby was taking her body through. He noticed how her face always held glowing and how her nose had spread a little. He even noticed the fact that her hair was a little thicker and carried a little more body than before. As he sat there and gazed at her for the tenth time he realized that she was the type of woman that looked good in under any condition.

He was draped in a grey pair of *Polo* jeans with a matching white long sleeve shirt with *Polo* imprinted in grey with a pair of blue and grey *Jordan's* on his feet. But what had her smiling from ear to ear was the Summer Street necklace he had around his neck.

"Deamon, what made you come and take me to lunch?" She asked with a wide grin.

"Dam, I really need a reason to take my lady to lunch?" He sarcastically questioned with a sly grin, "Baby girl, you know that we don't need any special occasions, cause whenever we're together it's special."

She was now blushing so hard that she had to look away from him. He smoothly reached over and grabbed her hand, causing her to look over at him. After seeing his serious expression she knew that he meant every word.

"You know I wanna take you somewhere so we can always enjoy each other without the outer interferences," she heard him say.

"Baby," she managed to stutter out, "you know that I'll go anywhere with you."

"Well, pick the spot."

"Baby, it wouldn't matter where we go, all I really wanna do is be with you," she replied as her eyes started to well up with tears, "so my spot is with you."

He raised from his seat and stepped to her before bending over and kissing her on the forehead and then the lips.

✱✱✱✱✱✱✱✱✱✱✱✱✱✱

Pimp, Black, Hamburger, Georgia Slim and Rip sat in a large booth inside of *Olive Garden.* They all was pretty high from the three blunts they had passed each other on their way to the restaurant in Pimp's Cadillac.

"Whose idea was it to come here?" Georgia Slim asked in a disgusted manner.

"What you tripping for!" Hamburger retorted, "Everything is everything on the menu."

"That might be so, but don't tell me you don't see all these eyes on us," he replied as he stuck his tongue out at one of the white women who sat at a table a few feet away from them.

"Playboy you just gotta get use to that," Rip stated with a chuckle, "muthafuckas gonna keep their eyes on us, we the hottest thing going right now."

"That's real," Pimp agreed, "I forgot Slim don't get out much. But since you're out, welcome to the life of a baller playboy," he added with a wide golden smile.

"You know I kind of dig the attention," Black stated, "it makes me realize how different we is from everybody else."

Hamburger smiled at the whole ordeal before stressing, "A nigga can't always look at things in a negative way, but to be real, I could careless what they looking at, I am about to slam into this pasta shit."

"What you about to order?" Black asked Hamburger.

"Some of everything big homie," he replied as he waved the waitress over before adding, "matter fact ya'll do the same, this shit on me."

Black was focused on the two women who had just walked in the restaurant before saying, "Say, ain't that Kruger's ole girl?"

All of the fellas focused on the females before Georgia Slim assured, "Yeah that's her, but I don't know who that is she with."

"Oh that's Ron's ole girl," Hamburger clarified, "you know she the one he got pregnant."

"Yes, may I help you sir?" The young, but cute, female asked Hamburger.

Hamburger looked up at her and smiled before replying, "I'm not really sure what I want, so can you bring me a sampler bowl of each of your most popular dishes?"

"Dam fool, you sound as if you're about to ask her if she has any *Grey Poupon*," Pimp stated causing all of the fellas and the waitress to burst out laughing. "Will that be all sir?" The waitress managed to giggle out.

"Could you make sure you bring enough to feed all of us?" He implied as he gave Pimp a cold stare.

"Yes sir," she replied as she regained her composure and asked, "and what would you like to drink?"

"I want some kool-aid or lemon-aid," he replied as he made eye contact with Teresa and waved her over before adding, "I don't know what they want."

Teresa and Toya both made their way over to the table as if they were models or something. As the fellas watched them sashay towards them each of their faces said that they enjoyed every moment of it.

"What's up Teresa, how you doing?" Hamburger greeted her.

"Hey, it's Hamburger right?" She replied as if she wasn't sure of who he was.

"Yeah, that's it," he replied with a wide grin that exposed his eighteen gold fronts.

"Have you met Ron's girl Toya?" Teresa asked.

"Now I know that Burger ain't the only one you see?" Black stressed.

"I apologize Black," she stated with a sly grin, "you know I was gonna speak to the rest of ya'll, but I guess I didn't get it out fast enough."

"You alright, that's really on Burger," he revealed as he pointed at the rest of the fellas and added, "but you do remember Rip, Slim and Pimp?"

"Hey fellas, how are ya'll doing?" She responded in a bashful manner.

"Dam, that nigga Ron got his girl on lock cause she don't say nothing in public," Pimp sarcastically stated.

"On a normal day I'd probably follow that up, but being that this is my chill day, I'm gonna let you slide with that," Toya stated with a smirk.

"I didn't mean any disrespect," Pimp stated as his eyes explored her body.

"I didn't detect any," she stressed before focusing on them as a whole and asking, "but how are ya'll doing?"

"We good, but how that baby doing?" Hamburger responded.

"Hell, how both of them babies doing?" Black added.

"They doing alright," Toya replied as she rubbed her stomach, "we just came here to feed their hungry asses."

"Well, eat whatever ya'll want, it's on me," Black insisted.

"I can't let you do that," Toya stressed as she looked over at Teresa, "I owe her lunch."

"That just means after today you'll still owe her," he rebutted with a sinister grin.

"I wish we had more room for ya'll to sit at the table with us, but ya'll know how that is," Hamburger stressed.

"Oh, we'll be alright," Teresa replied.

"Just remember it's on me, so she still owes you that lunch," Black stated as they started to walk towards the hostess.

"Thank-you Black," Toya replied.

"Boy that nigga Ron is definitely working with something," Pimp stressed as he watched her sashay away.

"Yeah, she is cute," Rip agreed.

"Man, if ya'll fools don't stop drooling over my homeboy's ole ladies I know something!" Black stressed right before the waitress came back to the table.

-KRUGER-

I read somewhere that in order to build oneness among the team, the general has to establish close kinship with those in branch. If it wasn't that exactly, I know that it was close to it. It also said without bonds of loyalty, punishment is felt only as pain. But with kinship established, punishment is understood as a matter of taking responsibility for one's action.

Since Slanga is locked-up, I'm forced to be the one to establish that kinship among the team, so I decided to treat all the fellas to the strip club tonight. Now, I don't know if that's what the author of that text had in mind, but I know what would put all the fellas on one accord.

I've already called all of them and told them to meet me at Dolls on 9th and Walton Way. I even invited Lil Dusty and Baby Gotti, I guess you can say I see some genuine traits in them two cats. Weasel and Jimmy said they was gonna roll through too, so it's really gonna be an interesting night.

Deidra just walked in the house with two huge grocery bags, looking sexy as ever. She know that she don't have no business carrying them heavy ass bags in here.

"Why didn't you call me to come get the bags out the car?" I asked as I took them from her and placed them on the island counter.

She just smiled and kissed me on the cheek before she tried to walk away.

"Now, you know that I can't have you teasing me like that," I stated as I pulled her back and buried my tongue in her mouth.

"So what time should I expect you home tonight?" She asked after our lips separated.

"With you tasting like that, I don't think that I'm going anywhere," I responded as I held her tightly.

"You already know that's what I want," she replied as she eased out of my grasp before adding, "help me put this food up, so I can get me before you leave here to go and see them strippers."

****

"*I thought* that fool said to be out here at 10:30," Hamburger stressed as him and the rest of the fellas stood outside of Dolls waiting on Kruger.

"Nigga calm down," Georgia Slim replied, "you know he'll be here in a minute."

"There go Mr. Bling-Bling," Pimp stated as he pointed towards the entrance, "you know he gotta come through like he the number one stunner."

"I swear to GOD that every time you open your mouth, it sounds as if you're hating just a little bit," Rip stressed as he walked over to the grill with Hamburger.

"Playboy, it ain't no hating in my blood!" He retorted, "I'm one of the realist cats you would ever run across!"

"Whatever fool, everybody knows that you have some shady ways," Black stepped up and stressed as he put his hand on Pimp's shoulder before he added, "we all have just accepted you for what you are."

All of the fellas just burst out laughing.

"What up my peoples?" Kruger stressed as he walked up and embraced everyone before asking, "Everybody know everybody, right?"

"Not really," Big Ox replied.

"Well, Ox," Kruger explained, "the only people you ain't familiar with is Lil Dusty and Baby Gotti and probably Fredel," he added as he pointed to all three of them.

STILL STUCK

"Now the reason that I got all of ya'll out here," Kruger continued as they all huddled around him, "is I wanted ya'll to know that these niggas ya'll see around you is the only ones I fuck with on a dirt level. So if a nigga say he fuck with me and he ain't here right now, you know he lying. With that said, I felt that all my niggas deserved at least one night from the streets with some cats that are on the same level they're on, and it's on me.

Now Baby Gotti and Lil Dusty are the young bucks of the crew so we probably have to sneak them in," he joked causing everyone to burst out laughing, "I'm just tripping kinfolk, but everyone just hold it down and like I said tonight's entertainment is on me."

An hour and a half later they all was in the VIP section smoking and drinking. Kruger sat on a couch in between Weasel and Jimmy smoking a blunt with a short haired six foot stallion dancing in front of them.

"You know I preciate you calling me up to be a part of this here," Weasel stressed to Kruger.

"You know that it ain't nothing homie, this is how it suppose to be and we both know that it's long overdue. I'm just doing it for the ones who don't know," Kruger explained.

"You right, because it ain't too many doing it like us."

"Na'll it ain't," Kruger agreed, "but that's because niggas are too busy trying to get over on each other, so they never see the big picture."

"You know I was serving them little cats Baby Gotti and Lil Dusty, but I lost sight of my priorities."

"So, is everything alright with you now?" Kruger asked in a concerned manner.

Weasel gave him one of those genuine smiles that you rarely see from men these days before he finally replied with, "Yeah my nigga, I'm good now."

From the lone look he saw on Weasel and Jimmy's faces Kruger knew that his little gathering was a good idea. Despite all the struggles a man may encounter in life, he knew that everything was much easier to deal with when you have a supporting cast.

****

Tamika and her future baby daddy was sitting on the couch watching television when Kruger walked in.

"What's up bra?" She stood up and embraced him.

"What up, you alright?" Kruger replied as he walked over to the couch.

"Yeah, I'm good," she assured him as she followed behind him in the kitchen, "but I have someone I want you to meet."

"Yeah, I heard," he stressed before he grabbed a glass of ice and walked back into the living room and stood in front of him.

Her future baby daddy had already stood up and now was looking Kruger dead in the eye before he greeted him, "What's up man, I'm Keenan."

He had his hand extended in a manly manner but Kruger looked him over and saw that he was nervous. To Kruger he wasn't his type of dude, but with him dealing with his sister, he felt that it was a good thing.

"Put your hand down," Kruger stressed before he walked passed him and sat on the love seat.

"Deamon, don't be acting ugly!" Tamika stressed while walking over and sitting next to him on the love seat.

"Mama meet this nigga yet?" He asked in a disgusting manner.

"Yes," she stated as she grabbed his arm in an attempt to calm him.

Kruger looked over at her and noticed that she was more nervous than her future baby daddy. He looked over at Keenan again and decided to eased both of their tensions.

"Say playboy, do you have any sisters?" He asked.

Keenan looked over at Tamika who wore a dumbfounded expression before he looked at Kruger and replied with, "Yeah, I got a little sister."

Kruger smiled at this before he asked, "Do she have a boyfriend yet?"

"Hell na'll, she too young!" Keenan retorted with aggression.

Kruger now wore a huge grin on his face before he stressed, "That's just how me and my peoples feel about Tamika, but obviously what's done is done. But you have to know that we're looking for you to treat her just like you would want a nigga to treat your little sister."

Without another word spoken he rose from the couch and walked down the hall to the bedroom where he heard the shower running. He walked past the shower and went and filled up his glass with his cognac.

After downing a glass and pouring another one he walked in the bathroom and asked, "How come everytime I come over here you're always in the shower?"

"Hey boo," she replied with a seductive smile as she peeked around the shower curtain.

"I just stopped through to speak," he stressed as he leaned against the sink, "I told you I had a few runs to make."

"Why do I get the feeling that you don't wanna talk to me?" She questioned from behind the shower curtain.

"Because you're under that steamy ass water and it has you thinking crazy as usual," he chuckled out.

"Ha, ha, ha," she sarcastically responded, "but if you have to go, I'm not gonna hold you up."

"Alright then," he stated before opening and closing the door as if he had left.

"Deamon!" She called his name as she slung the shower curtain open.

"Yeah, what up baby girl?" He replied with a sinister grin.

She couldn't help but giggle as she grabbed the towel from the rack and said, "I thought that you was about to leave without giving me a kiss."

"Is that all you want?" He questioned as he watched her dry off.

She gave him a look that said hell no, before she actually said, "I want whatever you want."

He smiled at this answer before he walked over and passionately kissed her. From the expression on his face after their lips separated, he was just as surprised at his actions as she was.

"So when am I gonna see you again, cause you know that the baby is gonna need to be fed soon," she questioned with her sexual look of hunger.

"Let me get at you about that a little later, I told you that I have to make some runs," he replied before he kissed her on the cheek and walked out of the bathroom.

As he walked down the hall he dug in his pocket, peeled off a hundred dollar bill, walked up and handed it to Tamika, "Ya'll take that and go and get something to eat, but make sure you bring Teresa something back."

"Preciate that bra," Tamika stressed.

He looked over at Keenan and said, "I just hope that you don't forget what I said."

****

Fredel sat on the couch while Baby Gotti was half asleep in the bedroom with his girl, Michelle. It was going on 11:30pm when Fredel heard the familiar knock at the door that let him know a customer was on their way to the back.

Fredel raised up, leaving the *Glock .40* that he normally took to the sliding door with him on the coffee table. When he slid the door open, two huge dudes, dressed in all black with ski-mask on, pointed pistols at him.

"Where it at?" The first one demanded to know.

"Man, what up?" Fredel managed to utter out.

The first guy just walked up to him and slapped him in the face with the pistol, causing Fredel to scream out in pain. He fell to his hands and knees from the hard blow as the blood started leaking from the side of his face.

Baby Gotti heard the unfamiliar noises from the front and quickly rolled out of the bed and grabbed the *SK* assault rifle from out of his closet.

"What's wrong Baby?" Michelle asked after realizing what he had in his hands.

"I don't know, but you just chill right here and I'll be right back," he stressed as he headed to the closed bedroom door.

Right before he opened the door he must have realized that it was a foolish move to go out that way, because he quickly turned his attention to the bedroom window.

In the living room Fredel was holding the left side of his face. The blow to the head must had affected his hearing because he couldn't hear a word the assailants was saying.

"I said where the dope at?" The first guy stated right before he kicked him in the face.

"Say," the second guy stressed as he tapped his partner on the arm.

"What up?" He asked in an agitated manner.

"Calm down for a minute fool!" The second guy practically demanded, "we need to check and see if anybody else in here!"

"Well what you still standing here for, handle that!" He responded before focusing back on Fredel.

Baby Gotti had already slipped out the window with his chopper in hand, so when he reached the sliding door all he saw was the first guy standing over Fredel. After seeing him kick Fredel in the ribs, he squeezed the trigger. The chopper's bullets penetrated through the sliding door glass and into the guy's back.

The second guy had already snatched up Michelle when he heard the shots. He quickly grabbed a hand full of her hair and pulled her towards the front. He was stopped in his tracks after seeing his partner laying on the floor moaning in a pool of blood.

After seeing Baby Gotti standing there holding the chopper he put his pistol to Michelle's head and demanded, "Put the gun down brave heart, before I blow this bitch's head off!"

"Sounds to me as if you've been watching too many movies," Baby Gotti replied with a sly grin before adding, "you actually think…"

That was all he was able to get out before some more shots were fired and he fell to the floor with the chopper still in hand.

"Nigga, what took you so long?" The guy holding Michelle asked the third assailant who'd just walked in holding Batman.

"I thought you niggas had this little bit under control," he responded as he pushed Batman to the ground, causing him to knock over the coffee table.

The one holding Michelle pushed her over to where the others were before grabbing his other partner who'd been shot and saying, "I'm gonna take this nigga to the car."

"You do that, while I make sure that we don't leave here empty handed," the third guy stated.

Fredel couldn't see the guys face but he knew that he was smiling under the mask he wore.

"Man, you might need to help me with this nigga, he heavy as hell," the other assailant stressed as he laid his moaning friend back on the floor.

The moment the third guy took his attention off their hostages, he heard multiple gun shots. Before they realized where the shots were coming from, they both fell to the floor.

"I know ya'll muthafuckas ain't think that shit was that sweet!" Fredel raised up and stressed with his *Glock .40* in hand, "Batman, get them guns from them hoes!"

Batman hesitated for a moment until Fredel turned on every light in the house.

"Chelle, you alright?" Fredel asked her as he stood over the assailants.

"I think so," she responded with tears flowing down her cheeks.

"Well, check on Baby Gotti," he stressed.

She crawled over toward him as she continued to call out his name.

"Chelle," he managed to whine out, "you alright?"

"Yeah, what about you?" She answered.

"Na'll," he replied with blood coming out the corner of his mouth, "my back is killing me."

"We gotta get him to the hospital," Fredel implied.

"Where the keys to the car at?" She asked in a frantic manner.

"They're on the kitchen counter," Fredel replied before adding, "Batman, call the police."

He then walked over to the three assailants and pulled their mask's off before stressing, "Say Gotti, you won't believe who one of these cats is?"

"Enlighten me," Baby Gotti managed to say.

"It's that nigga Rock," he replied right before he kicked him in the face.

"Shiesty ass nigga," Baby Gotti managed to spat out.

"Dam that nigga, we gotta get you to the hospital like yesterday," Fredel stressed as he helped him up before looking over at Batman and stressing, "I thought I told you to call the folks!"

-KRUGER-

Now here I am pulling up at the hospital and I can't even find a parking spot. I wonder why ain't nobody call me last night. It looks like I'm the last one here, cause I see Burger's truck, Pimp's Caddy and Slim's black Northstar he just coped. Hell, here go Jimmy pulling up behind me, and there we have it, two open parking spaces.

"What up playboy?" I greeted as I walked up and embraced him.

"Just coming to see what the business is with the little homie," he replied before activating his car alarm.

"That's respect right there," I replied as we walked towards the entrance.

As we were walking in the lobby, the rest of the fellas were walking out with sorrowful expressions.

"What up?" I asked with mad concern.

"He resting right now," Lil Dusty answered with a look of anguish.

"How did the surgery go?" Jimmy asked.

"Good, I guess. The doctor say one of the bullets missed his heart by less than an inch," Lil Dusty replied.

"You alright?" I just had to ask the little homie.

"I'm just ready to rectify this shit!" Is all he stressed.

"Well, let's talk about it at a restaurant on me," Jimmy jumped in and stressed.

I'm glad that he stepped up and handle it like that, cause little homie is about to explode, and who could really blame him.

"You ride with me Dust," I urged as we made our way to our vehicles.

Moments later me Black and Lil Dusty were trailing Jimmy's Infiniti, with the other fellas trailing me.

"So, what is it you wanna do?" I asked the little homie.

"Man, you already know what I wanna do!" He replied with this devilish expression.

"So where they at?" Black asked from the backseat.

"They say that two of them are in ICU at *MCG*, and that nigga Rock is in 401, but he in the infirmary."

"So how you gonna touch them?" Black questioned.

"I can't call that right now, but them niggas have to be dealt with!"

"I can feel where you're coming from homie, but you have to be patient. You know we down with you, but it ain't no need in pulling no foolish moves to jeopardize the family," I stated causing Lil Dusty to give me a bewildered expression.

"Yeah, fool," I added with a sly grin, "ya'll considered family now."

When I looked in the rear-view at Black he gave me the head nod of approval I'd been looking for.

"Ya'll know that nigga Rock was at the strip club the other night," Lil Dusty revealed.

"We wouldn't know cause we ain't never laid eyes on the nigga," Black reminded him.

"I know," he stressed in a depressed manner, "but he tried to get in VIP with us, but I told him that it was a private party. I guess that's when I feel the nigga caught animosity."

"Playboy, don't take that shit to heart," I stressed to him to comfort him a little, "it's obvious that the nigga been hating."

With that said I just turned up the sounds of 8-Ball and MJG's, *'Friend or Foe'* and let them niggas give it to him raw.

(CHAPTER 9)

Rip, Black, Hamburger, Georgia Slim and Kruger sat in the middle room of 1122 watching the movie, *Sugerhill.*

"This cat Wesley Snipes know he playing in all types of movies," Rip implied as he sipped on a cup of *Hennessy.*

"Yeah," Black agreed, "but I don't think he can ever play a better part than Nino Brown."

"Hell, the nigga tight in this one," Kruger stressed, "I like the way he be thinking."

"If you think about it, this is nothing but an upgrade of *Superfly*," Hamburger implied after taking a long pull from the blunt in his hand, "Romelo is trying to get out the game just like Preacher was."

"I ain't never looked at it like that, but that's just what it is," Kruger agreed as he reached for the blunt that Hamburger was passing him.

"My nigga, I've been thinking about that too, cause you know we can't trap for the rest of our lives," Rip revealed.

"Point definitely seen," Kruger agreed.

"I'm feeling that too," Hamburger added, "but it ain't no money like dope money."

"My nigga, look at how Romelo lost all of his people to the game and still ended up in a wheel chair," Georgia Slim implied, "sometimes a nigga just gotta sit and ask himself is it really worth it."

"That's just how shit go!" Kruger assured, "If a playa stay in the game long enough, it's almost guaranteed that we'll experience a lot of bullshit. But the crazy thing about all of that is, we already know it and we're still in it, waist deep."

Georgia Slim nodded his head in agreement before stressing, "We already know what's-what, it's them dudes out here who thinking shit sweet, they the ones that's fucking shit up!"

"That's been understood, but what the hell are we suppose to do about it?" Rip questioned right before Kruger's phone started ringing.

"What up bra?" Ron stated through the receiver after Kruger answered.

"What's up my nigga, I haven't heard from you in a minute," he responded.

"Man, I've been working."

"So what's up then, you alright?"

"Yeah I'm good, but I'm in the hospital with Teresa."

"For what?!"

"She got in an accident on her way to work this morning."

"What hospital?"

"University."

"I'll be there in a minute," he stated before pushing the end button.

Hamburger saw the distant expression he held and asked, "Is everything alright?"

"Man Teresa done got in an accident," he replied in a sadden tone as he walked out the room towards the front door.

"I'm gonna ride with you," he stated as he followed him.

They rode in silence the entire way to the hospital. When they finally reached the lobby of the emergency room, Kruger noticed Ron and Toya sitting in the waiting area.

"So what's the word?" He walked up and asked.

Toya just looked up at him with tears flowing down her cheeks.

"Is she alright or what?" He asked in an impatient manner.

"Let me hollar at you over here," Ron stressed to his brother as he raised from his seat.

He pulled his brother over by the restroom area while Hamburger sat down and comforted Toya.

"So what's up?" He asked Ron again.

"First of all calm down my nigga, she alright," he replied.

"So where are all the tears coming from if she's so alright?!" He demanded to know.

"She lost the baby my nigga," he practically whispered out, "she hit head on with a truck and it pushed the steering wheel closer to her, so when the air bag shot out, it shot out with too much force."

"Dam," Kruger spat out before he walked away and into the bathroom with his brother right behind him.

"You alright lil bra?" He asked after the door closed behind him.

"So how she doing?" He asked as he stared at himself through the mirror.

"She straight, she just had a few bump and bruises and a broken arm."

"They ain't let nobody see her?" Kruger asked as the tears flowed down his face.

"Yeah, but I didn't let Toya go in," he replied as he stepped closer and put his hand on his little brother's shoulder, "I told her that was for you to do first."

"Preciate that," Kruger stated as he turned around and embraced him.

"You know it ain't nothing my nigga," he replied as they embraced, "but is you gonna be alright?"

"Yeah playboy," he replied with a sly grin as they broke apart.

"Nigga, wipe your face, cause you can't go out there like that, you Kruger, my nigga! Plus, you know you have to be strong for the both of ya'll, cause you know she's gonna be crying when she see you."

"True," he replied as he wiped his face with the back of his hand.

"Here," Ron stressed as he handed him some tissue, "everything is gonna be everything , my nigga."

"Yeah, this just some more bullshit a playa gotta deal with," he responded with before walking out of the bathroom with his brother behind him.

"Say Toya," he called out as he walked towards her and Hamburger who were talking with a nurse.

Toya quickly turned her attention from the nurse and looked over at Kruger who was now walking towards them.

"Huh," she replied.

"Do you know what room she's in?"

"You must be Deamon?" The nurse asked with a friendly smile.

"Yeah, that's me," he replied.

"Well, Teresa has been asking for you, so you can follow me," she replied before leading him to a glass door that led down a long hallway.

"Are you alright?" She asked after stopping him in the middle of the hallway.

Kruger then took a second to look at the nurse. She was a shade lighter than himself with her hair pinned up. If she was a little thinner he felt that she looked just like Deidra.

"Yes mamm, I'm alright," he replied with a smile of his own.

"Please sir, don't call me mamm, that makes me feel as if I'm getting old or something," she flirted before walking up the hall.

"I can only oblige if you stop calling me sir, you know my name," he replied as he followed her.

"You have a deal," she stated, "by the way my name is Rebecca, but you can call me Becky."

A few moments later they had stopped in front of a door labeled, ER rm. 26, Teresa Davis. Becky reached out to open the door before Kruger stopped her.

"I think I can handle it from here," he stated with a cool smile.

She gave him a warm smile before saying, "Very well Deamon. If you need me I'll be in room 22."

When he walked in the room he saw that Teresa was asleep. She had her head wrapped in a gauze, along with a few minor cuts on her face and neck. Her right eye was swollen, but besides that, she looked like Teresa.

"Teresa," he whispered as he grabbed her hand that wasn't wrapped in a cast.

Her body jerked before she opened her left eye. That's when he realized that she couldn't open her right eye.

"Deamon," she whispered with an expression that he couldn't tell if it was relief or grief.

"Yeah, it's me," he stated with a light smile before adding, "I got word that you was looking for me."

She attempted to smile but he could tell that it was painful for her.

"My bad baby girl," he apologized, not knowing what else to say.

"Are you alright?" She asked in a concerned manner as she tried to sit up.

He never answered her as he helped her get comfortable.

"So when they say they gonna let you come home?" He finally asked after a brief moment.

"They haven't told me yet," she replied with a sad expression.

"Well, I'm taking you to Savannah so that your mama can help nurse you back to normal," he stated in a comforting manner.

"I don't wanna go there, I wanna stay here with you," she replied as she grabbed his hand.

He smiled at her before replying, "I'm gonna stay with you a few days, but you're going to Savannah."

She just pulled her hand from his closed her eyes and asked, "So how long?"

"How long what?" He asked in a confused manner.

"How long have you been trying to get rid of me?" She questioned as she looked at him, "And don't lie to me Deamon, because I've seen it

332

in your eyes for a while. I guess you can say that I was in denial."

"Do you really think we need to be talking about this right now?" He asked as he saw the tears rolling down her cheeks.

"Will you just tell me dammit!" She stressed with aggression, "I'm a big girl, you can tell me."

"Chill out baby girl," he pleaded with her, "there is a time and place for everything, and this isn't the time or place."

"Better time or place than any! Have you heard about your baby?"

"Yeah, I heard," he managed to utter out as he walked away from the bed.

"So why didn't you come in here talking about that?" She blasted, "At least I would've known that you knew!"

He turned to face her and she could see that he was mourning just as much as she was, "Listen Teresa, you must understand that I bleed just like you bleed. I have feelings and shit too. This is my first time going through some shit like this, but if you had a script that I'm supposed to be reading from, you should've gave it to the nurse to give me. But since there isn't one, I'm standing here giving you me, but obviously that isn't enough."

He then turned to walk out the room.

"Deamon," she called out, "I'm sor, I mean I apologize. Dam! See how you got me fucked up? It's like I can't even be myself around you. Sometimes, I just feel so uncomfortable. Hell, it's like I have to act out a script to be with you too."

He then walked back over to her bed and grabbed her hand again, "Do you remember what you use to tell me you wanted to be when I was locked up?"

She sat there with a confused expression before he continued, "You use to tell me how successful you wanted to be. You use to tell me about your dreams, the places that you wanted to go, the type of people you wanted to meet and the type of company you wanted to keep. Do you remember that?"

She just nodded her head in agreement. At that moment she realized where a lot of their problems had come from.

"Now whatever happened to that woman?" He questioned, "Sometimes, I believe that she only exist in the back of your mind, and I hate that because that's the woman I fell for. Now every promise that I made to you, I kept, even when I felt I wasn't ready for it."

"So why didn't you say something?"

"The excuses that I have ain't even worth me speaking on, besides, I think you already know."

"So I guess this is it?" She asked.

He looked at her and shook his head before stressing, "You know that me and you are always gonna be cool. I mean there isn't any bad blood between us, well, at least not from me."

"Don't you know that I've been dreading this day for months," she stated with a light smile, "but I'm glad that's it's out in the open though."

He leaned over and pecked her on the lips as she tightened her grip on his hand.

"So when are we leaving for Savannah?" She asked with a positive attitude.

****

Baby Gotti was laying on the couch while Michelle changed the dressing on his back. She was already scolding him about all the smoking and drinking he was doing, but he really wasn't paying her any attention.

He was laying there thinking about the night he got shot. There wasn't a doubt in his mind that he wanted Rock and the other two assailants dead, but he knew that they had too much security around them.

"How you feeling boo?" Michelle finally asked after applying the medicated lubricate.

"I'm good," he replied with a sly grin, "you know those pain pills have me at ease."

"I can't see how they working with you still doing all that smoking and drinking," she responded as she slapped the back of his head.

"I can't see you playing me like that," he replied with a light chuckle before asking, "you heard from Tiffany and Dust?"

"Yeah, they should be on their way over here so they can get in that kitchen and cook us something to eat."

"If you think Lil Dusty about to cook, you might as well order some pizza," he managed to chuckle out.

"Well, I'll just help her cook," she assured him.

"That ain't no better!" He retorted, "It takes ya'll days to fry chicken," he added with a laugh so overwhelming that his back started hurting.

"I hope your ass is hurting all over, with your ungrateful ass!" She stressed as she finished bandaging him up.

"Why you tripping, you know I'm just playing," he responded with a smile as he sat up.

"Na'll, your ass was dead serious!" She blasted as she stomped towards the bedroom.

Baby Gotti just smiled to himself because he already knew she wanted him to follow her, "I hate your black ass!" She added as he walked in the room behind her.

"Stop lying, you know you love the hell out of me," he replied in a humble manner as he pushed her on the bed.

She saw the lust in his eyes as he climbed over her turning her on more than anything. He buried his tongue in her mouth with so much eagerness that she was flushed with emotions. Her love for him had went to that ultimate peak when he cared more for her then himself the night he got shot. After that, she knew that she was with him forever.

After seeing the tears flowing down her cheeks he asked, "You alright baby girl?

She just stared at him for a moment before replying with, "You know I'll die for you, don't you?"

He just gazed down at her for a moment with a broad smile before replying with, "Boo, I don't need you to die for me, I just need you to live with me."

****

"Ron, I really don't appreciate how your brother is doing Teresa," Toya was implying after she finished brushing her teeth.

"So what you want me to do about it?" He asked with his head under the cover.

"You don't have to get all jazzy!" She retorted.

"I'm just saying," was his response as he pulled the covers from over his face, "from what I hear, they both agreed that this is what they were gonna do. So, I really can't see why you can't accept it."

"That doesn't make it right!" She stressed as she sat on the side of the bed, "She gets in a car wreck and he throws her back to another city with her mama. The nigga ain't even show any emotions about the lost of his child!"

Ron quickly sat up before blasting, "First of all, you need to mind your dam business! That's my brother you're talking about! Your silly ass don't know how he felt, cause you on the outside looking in! You need to check yourself cause shit be bigger than what your little eyes can capture!"

He then crawled out of bed and added, "You're nothing but a selfish ass bitch! Instead of looking at both of their points of view, you chose to create your own, and it ain't even your problem!"

She just sat there staring at him with a shocked expression before she started to say, "I was just saying.."

"I know what your wanna be GOD ass was just saying!" He interrupted, "But you still haven't realized that you can't control everything."

"This sounds as if it's a little bigger than Teresa and Deamon," she implied with a confused expression.

He gave her a sinister expression before taking a deep breath and replying with, "You right, it is. It's about how you look at shit. I mean, did you ever think about how they been dragging each other in that relationship? This might be what they need."

"Well, why wait until now, after she has lost her baby?"

"Maybe that's just something you need to ask her," he replied as he walked in the bathroom.

"Why haven't you asked Deamon?"

"Either you're mental health or you just don't comprehend quick enough," he managed to chuckle out, "but that ain't my business."

"Well, Teresa is my girl! It's my job to make sure she straight, so don't try to tell me that I'm doing something wrong," she stressed as she raised from the bed and was about to exit the room before he stopped her.

"And what was she when you dragged her with you to Savannah to see them other dudes?" He asked as he peeked out of the bathroom with a sly grin, "Besides, looking out for your, quote on quote girl, is one thing, but tripping on my little brother is another."

****

"Say bra," Tamika was asking Kruger, "you really gonna let her go like that?"

They were sitting in the living room with Keenan, while Teresa was in the bathroom taking a bath.

"I tried to tell her to chill for a minute at least until she gets back on her feet, but you know how she is," he replied in a disappointed manner.

"If you really wanted her to stay, you could've came up with a better way to ask her," Tamika implied with a gruesome expression.

"So what you want me to do, act as if we still have a chance, when I know we don't," he replied in a sorrowful tone, "Don't get it twisted I have mad love for her, and she knows that, but we're on two different stations and I can't keep turning the channel to hers, because I'll eventually end up missing something on mine."

"Now that's some real shit!" Keenan stressed after he really thought about what Kruger had just said.

Kruger smiled at the complement while Tamika looked over at him with a cold stare.

"You need to go and talk to her because you're stupid ass can't send her home all scared up like that!" She stressed with aggression before implying, "Now how would you feel if Keenan sent me home like that?"

Kruger looked over at his little sister, who obviously wasn't that little anymore, before he looked over at Keenan, who just shrugged his shoulders. He then raised from the love seat and walked to the bathroom door.

"Teresa, can I come in?" He asked after knocking on the door.

"Of course."

After walking in and gazing at her for a moment, he realized that Tamika was more than right. Teresa's arm was still in the cast and she still had a black eye.

He kneeled at the edge of the tub before saying, "You know that I really don't want you to leave like this."

"But you do want me to leave?" She asked as if nothing else mattered.

"On the real, I don't," he stated before taking a deep breath and adding, "you have been a big part of my life for a minute now, so it's hard for me to let you go like this. The thing is, I don't want us working on a future together, because that's how we got in this position. I wanna see you grow, and you haven't been able to do that with me. I want you to grasp those goals you use to feed me when I was locked-up."

This obviously made her feel better because she was smiling from ear to ear.

"There isn't a doubt in my mind that you can do this for you," he continued, "but you need to want it for yourself again. Me and you started as good friends and that's how I want us to always be. So as a good friend, I'm asking you stay until we can get you right."

****

"Have you heard from Slanga?" Kay-Kay was asking Big Ox as they sat on the couch in Gunslanga's trap smoking a blunt.

"Na'll, but I heard he should get out at his preliminary hearing," he replied with a cloud of smoke seeping from his nose and mouth.

"I hope he gets out for real," she stated in a sincere manner.

"Like I said he should, but you know how them crackers be switching shit up. It's gonna be wild to see how this shit plays out."

"I thought they didn't have any evidence on him since that boy changed his statement?"

"Say ya'll," Vader calmly said through the window, "we have company."

"Dam, its Honeycutt them!" Big Ox stressed after peeking out the window.

"You got something in here?" She asked him.

344

"Yeah, I got like two ounces in this muthafucka!" He confessed.

"Well, you need to throw that shit back there with them dogs!" She yelled.

Big Ox scurried through the small house. The moment he threw the dope as far as he could and walked back in the house, six agents had their pistols pointed at him.

"Get your bitch ass on the ground, now!" One of them yelled.

He quickly scanned the room to see where Kay-Kay was before he noticed her already on the floor between the sofa and coffee table.

"You must don't hear too well clown!" Another agent stressed as he eased closer to Big Ox.

Big Ox quickly raised his hands and laid on the ground before mumbling, "I know your mama taught you better manners than that."

That's when another one of the agents stepped over him and kicked him in the side of the head before implying, "I know you ain't talking about my mama!"

"Dead man walking," Big Ox managed to say with his hand over his freshly bloody wound.

"What you say, boy!" The same agent who kicked him violently asked.

"I said, how does it feel to be a dead man walking, bitch!" He retorted.

He kicked Big Ox on the side of the face before stressing, "You can't know who your fucking with!"

The kick seemed as if it didn't even faze him as he positioned himself on his hands and knees before he spearheaded the agent out of the front door. Big Ox landed on top of the agent and started unloading vicious punches to his face.

"Na'll bitch, you don't know who you fucking with!" He managed to utter through clinched teeth as he continued to deliver powerful blows.

The other agents were obviously unprepared because it took them a moment before they even attempted to restrain Big Ox.

Black, Pimp and Hamburger had just made it down from 1122 and without a thought they went right to Big Ox's defense with. Black quickly grabbed the officer who had his knee to the back of Big Ox's neck and slung him to the ground. The other officers quickly raised their guns at Black.

"Now ya'll know if ya'll shoot him, it's a must ya'll shoot me first!" Hamburger nervously stated as he walked between Black and the pistol with his hands raised.

Big Ox raised up from the ground with streams of blood coming from his forehead and left eye before he stressed, "Ya'll obviously ain't do your homework on this shit here!"

"What you gonna do Honeycutt?" Pimp questioned with a golden smile as he stood next to his comrades, "You in check, but you can check-mate us right here in front of all these beautiful people."

Honeycutt just smiled at the hoodlums before saying, "All of ya'll are getting locked-up for obstruction of an officer, put your hands behind your back."

"For what?" Big Ox asked, "For one of ya'll muthafuckas to kick me in my face again?!"

Honeycutt gave his agents a disgruntled expression before finally looking back at Big Ox with an genuine response, "I didn't know that it was going down like that, and you have my word that it would be taken care of."

-KRUGER-

Here I am in the backseat of a rented Navigator, with a 5th of *Hennessy* in my lap and a blunt in my mouth, with Amanda driving and Deidra in the passenger seat. They're up there laughing and chatting about something, I really don't have the patience to be listening to, cause I'm already on deck with enough issues.

With all that's going on in my life I definitely feel as a huge mountain has been lifted off my shoulders with Teresa. I ain't saying that I'm happy that she lost the baby, hell, that's like the worst news a warrior could ever receive. But I am happy that me and her has an understanding now.

There is no fun in a relationship that was built of dreams. Especially when both parties aren't totally invested in committing their ends of the bargain. There is no doubt that I have mad love for Teresa, but I stopped investing in that relationship a long time ago.

I'm extremely proud of myself for finally letting her know how I really feel about the situation. She even confessed the fact that David and Toya has been trying to put her on point. I don't know about Toya though, I feel she's just as shady as they come, but that's something Teresa and bra has to deal with.

I wanted to hit her with the David situation, but I had already hit her with so much other shit, that to bring that up would probably be pouring it on a little too thick. I'm more enthused about the fact that she's working more on herself than us, she really deserves better.

Well I finally got on this road to go and holler at Firebug. I need some wise words these days. I hate the fact that we riding with all this cheddar though, shit really just don't feel right.

Here go this phone ringing again.

"Yeah, get at me," I answered.

"Hey Kruger, this Kay-Kay."

"What up?" I asked as I looked up at Deidra who was acting as if she wasn't paying me any attention, or maybe I was just paranoid because I'm already knowing that I done knocked this broad off.

"The narcs just hit the house and took Black, Burger, Ox and Pimp to jail."

"They found dope on them again?"

"Na'll, they tried to jump on Ox and Black them came down here and stopped them so them folks locked them all up for obstruction."

"They bust Slanga's house?" I questioned.

"Yeah, they had a search warrant and all, but they never got a chance to search for nothing cause they got to hooking with Ox."

I couldn't help but smile at the thought of Ox tussling with the police before I told her to call up to booking to see what their bonds are and hit me back. To keep it genuine all of this getting locked up and shit for the birds. My niggas get locked up every dam month, shit can't be this bad everywhere.

"Is there anything you need me to do?" Deidra turned around in her seat and asked me.

"Na'll boo," he replied before stressing, " do you know them muthafuckas tried to jump on Ox?"

"Who?" Amanda asked as if she was ready for war.

"Honeycutt and his band of misfits, but Black and the rest of the fellas went down there and stopped that shit. So now they locked up for obstruction."

"Felony or misdemeanor?" Deidra asked.

"I don't even know, but Kay-Kay suppose to call me back to let me know something."

"Some shit stay happening on the Summer," Amanda spat out.

"I know right," I replied with a frustrated expression before I took a pull from the blunt and a deep gulp of the cognac.

I watched as Deidra unbuckled her seat belt and climb in the back with me before saying, "I thought you probably needed me a little closer to you."

I put the blunt out in the ash-tray on the side panel before I pecked her on the lips and replied, "Sometimes it seems as if me and you are the only thing working these days."

I don't know what made me look up in the rear-view mirror, but that's when I saw Amanda smiling at the way we were carrying on. The next thing I heard was *Mary J. Blige* album blasting through the speakers.

****

Fredel was outside tending to the meat on the grill when his phone started vibrating on his hip.

"Fredel's," he responded with a cool smile.

"What up cuz, this Kay-Kay?"

"What up Ms. Hustler?"

"Man, Black and them just got locked up for fighting with the police."

"Them niggas crazy for real ain't they!" He replied as if he couldn't believe it.

"That's what I said."

"You got at Kruger yet?"

"Yeah, he told me to see how much their bonds were and hit him back, but they ain't even been processed yet."

"Well, hit me back before you hit Kruger, cause me, Dust and Gotti might go scoop them."

"Alright cuz," she stated right before the line went dead.

Fredel walked in the house where Lil Dusty and Baby Gotti were sitting on the couch smoking a blunt and gave them the news. Before he could imply about getting them out, Baby Gotti opened his mouth.

"We can get them fools out!" He stated with a concern expression, "They were there for me when I caught them slugs, now it's time to show that love back."

"Kay-Kay suppose to be calling me back so I'll let her know then," Fredel responded with a smile of approval.

"Them niggas gonna trip when they find out that we the ones that got them out," Lil Dusty stressed with a smile of his own.

"Know they ain't," Baby Gotti rebutted, "they just gonna realize why Kruger had us all meet."

"Real niggas do real things!" Fredel stressed as he lit the end of a blunt.

"I'm like that nigga Kruger now," Lil Dusty stressed, "that real shit ain't good enough for me these days. So genuine dudes commit genuine deeds!"

"Yeah," Baby Gotti stated with a smile of his own, "I'm really feeling that."

STILL STUCK

Kruger and Firebug sat at their regular table inside of Longhorn's on Abercorn, while Deidra and Amanda was strolling through the city with the twins. Kruger had just told Firebug about the few mishaps he'd been having the past few weeks.

"Dam young blood," Firebug responded with a sincere expression, "I'm sorry to hear about you losing your seed like that. Shit like that makes a man wonder if it really was meant for you."

"At first I really didn't know how to react to the news, and I hated that because it showed," Kruger stated as if he was disappointed with himself.

"Well you can't beat yourself in the head about it," he informed in a cool manner before taking a sip of his cognac before adding, "somethings come natural. With us being human and all, we don't have control over shit like we would want. For the ones who know we don't, take our tribulations with a smile. You been locked-up before, so I know you're familiar with the saying, do the time and don't let it do you."

Kruger nodded in acknowledgement.

"See you have to bring that same attitude out here on these bricks, especially when dealing with these bricks. The only thing different from in there and out here is you have to bring more determination out here. You already know how I felt about Wade."

Kruger looked at him thoroughly before nodding his head again.

"Well, I would have never thought in a million years that he would've crossed me the way he did, but it happened. It had me down for a second, but that was all the time I could afford to give it. The way that I looked at it, if I would have gave it a second more, it could have easily turned from a trial to my demise."

Kruger was keened in on Firebug's every word, "I can see where you're coming from."

"And another thing," Firebug stated after taking another sip of his cognac, "you have to stop putting so much time and energy into your peoples."

"What you talking about?" Kruger asked openly disturbed by the comment.

Firebug noticed the puzzled expression but still pressed on, "I'm just saying, every time that something goes wrong with them you try to be right on top of the shit."

"With me even claiming friends, that's what I'm supposed to do!" He retorted.

"That's true and I respect your loyalty towards them, but all of those unnecessary commotions is draining the hell out of you. Besides you're taking away from them growing when you always there. You know what you need? You look as if you're in need of a vacation."

"Pop's, you know that I don't have time for a vacation, not now anyway."

"See, that's what I'm talking about," he responded as he reclined in his seat, "you're so concerned about everyone else that you're neglecting the most important person, and that's the cat you see in the mirror every morning."

"You know that I'm taking care of me!" Kruger retorted.

"You can't be," he replied in a calm manner, "we done been here for thirty to forty-five minutes and you done drunk four glasses of cognac to my one. See, all I'm asking you to do is calm down young blood, cause I need you out here with me. Right now, we're in a position where we don't have to chase nothing, in due time, everything we want or need comes knocking at our door. You have to learn to pace yourself."

"I guess I can try and slow shit down a little," he replied with a sly grin.

"Don't worry, I'm gonna help you out a little," he replied with a smirk.

"How is that?"

"I ain't gonna serve you until Wednesday or Thursday, so you have three or four days to get your thoughts together."

"What about the people I have waiting on me?"

"I guess they have a little longer wait, huh?"

-TERESA-

Back to square one!

Here I am laying across this bed with my arm in a cast. It's still hard to believe that I lost my child and my man over the weekend. Who the hell am I fooling, I been lost Deamon. I was just too afraid to accept the reality of it all.

I don't know what's up with me and these car wrecks. That's why I was so reluctant to head back to Savannah. Lord knows that I don't wanna hear my mama's mouth, I'm already catching hell with Toya in my ear. I know they both mean well, but I'm not into the motivational speeches these days.

Between Toya and Tamika I'm being treated like a queen in here. They've been waiting on me hand to feet. But to be honest, I think that they're just more relieved that it wasn't them who was under the wheel, and I can't really blame them for that.

Here it is twenty minutes after midnight and somebody is calling me.

"What's up baby-girl, how you doing?" I hear Deamon's voice.

Dam, I wish I had him here to cuddle with.

"Hey stranger, how you doing?"

It ain't no way I'm gonna let him know that I'm missing him like crazy.

"I'm good, but have you ate?"

"Yeah, Toya came through after she got off and fixed some spaghetti."

"That was nice of her," he replied.

I can hear it in his voice that he really don't care too much for Toya these days.

"Well, I was just calling to see if you were alright, you know I didn't mean to wake you," I heard him say.

The same ole Deamon. He's always trying to run me off the phone.

"I wasn't sleep, I was just laying here thinking."

"What you thinking about?" He asked.

"Everything," I replied in a sorrowful tone.

I wasn't trying to sound helpless or anything, but when I really thought about my predicament, how else was I suppose to feel. I hated the fact that everything around me seems to always be seconds away from leaving.

"So are you thinking in a negative or a positive way?" I heard him ask.

Like I said, I wasn't trying to sound all helpless, but I couldn't hold back the tears. They just ran down my cheeks like water running out of the faucet.

"Deamon, I really don't know how to think anymore," I cried out.

The phone was silent as if he was crying himself, but I knew that bad ass Kruger holds no tears.

"Baby girl," I heard him practically whisper, "you know I have your back in anything you wanna accomplish."

"I know, but I'm just tired of starting over," I continued to cry out, "It's scary not knowing what your next move is gonna be."

"You can't look at it as if you're starting over, you have to look at it as if you're moving on. You can't look at our situation like you've lost me because I'm still active and very relevant in your life as long as you'll have me."

I wanted to tell him that I wanted him in my life forever. I wanted to tell him that my love for him could never be tarnished. I wanted to let him know that I'm nothing without him, but for some reason it never rolled off my tongue.

Instead I found myself saying, "Well, let me get off this phone, because I know you have more important things to deal with."

"Alright then," he replied, but I could tell that he wasn't really ready to hang up.

"Call me if you miss me again," I managed to giggle out.

He laughed to before replying with, "Yeah, I gotcha."

When I hung that phone up, I realized that it would take a lifetime to get over somebody like him. But I also realized that I would really be a fool to try to hold on to someone or anything that's already dead. That's just dead weight, and I already have enough shit I'm carrying around. When it all boils down, I realize that I have to start thinking about Teresa again.

(CHAPTER 10)

-KRUGER-

Firebug done practically introduced me to every high roller in Savannah, on the east, west and south sides. It was this one cat he put me on that fuck with that dogg food. Pop say that he good people, but with Big Wade in mind, I'm still going to keep my eyes open.

I really gotta see how he operates before I get at him with what I got. I think I'll be better off coping a half ounce from him just to see what he working with and go from there. Me and Firebug suppose to get with him later on tonight.

Its Wednesday and Halloween is Friday, so me and the girls are hitting the road in the morning. Firebug don't want me to leave just yet, but I have too much to handle at home right now. Besides, I have to see my parole officer Monday morning.

I'll be lying if I said that I was ready to leave, because Firebug has showed me nothing but love. Everywhere we went he was pulling my coat to one thing or the other.

"Youngblood, keep your eyes on every cat in here," is what he might say. "If you can look in their faces, try to see what their eyes are saying. Because believe me, you have more enemies then you're aware of!"

Now I can feel where he was coming from considering what he'd been through, but to me he was just being paranoid. The way I'm thinking, if I spend all my time focusing on how another cat is perceiving me, then I won't have time to concentrate on the business at hand.

But when I stressed that to him, he hit me with, "Your business is gonna handle itself. Your mind don't be so far gone that you'll spend a grand on a plain t-shirt. Besides, you have to learn to chew gum and walk at the same time."

Now that's respect!

I can tell that Deidra has been a little jealous of how me and Pop been kicking it, cause me and her hasn't spent much time together. Her and Amanda has been staying at our hotel room with the twins. This morning she told me that the twins say Firebug hasn't been this energetic in a long time, so I guess my stay was for the better on both of our behalf.

STILL STUCK

Considering the situation with Teresa, she's doing a lot better than she was at first. I guess time does heal all wounds.

Everything seems to be back to normal down the way, but shit is bound to blow over at any time. Hopefully, Slanga gets out next Friday, so he can put some of this weight on his shoulders.

Hammah called me yesterday asking about Teresa. He say he heard that she got into an accident on her way to work. I hit him with the news, and naturally he gave his condolences and all. I just wish my nigga was out here to help get this paper.

Dust and Gotti been calling me all day screaming that I need to get home. Those two cats has some good hearts. I love the way they stepped up and handle the situation with the fellas.

As I sit here waiting on Deidra to come through so we can spend at least one night together, I realize that these few days really did me some good. Now I feel as if I'm well rested and more focused to handle whatever.

****

Honeycutt stood in front of his 14 or so agents inside the narcotic division of the Augusta precinct. It was Thursday afternoon around one o'clock and he was going over the few house warrants he'd just persuaded the judge to sign.

"Listen fellas," he was saying, "we have four stings we have to pull today. Now there is no way we can have what went down on Summer Street earlier this week, happen today. Now, I've been giving the word that a few of my guys has dishonored the oath they pledge to this department, and those who have, already know who you are," he stressed as he paced back in forth in front of them.

"Now, if you know that you're involved in these unjust agreements with the enemy," he continued before pausing and glaring at Sanchez and Olgetree, before adding, "now if you have forgotten who the enemy is, let me refresh your memory. The enemy is these punks who flood our streets with poison, whether it's heroine or a dime bag of weed. The enemy doesn't have to distribute it himself either. He could even inform these same punks about when we're coming.

Now, it's really hard for me to stand here and believe that any of my men could've violated

365

such an oath. I mean I personally handpicked you all. But it has been brought to my attention that no man knows what the power of greed!" He stated with aggression as he stopped in front of Martin.

"I know that our salaries aren't up to par, and yeah, we're out here risking it all for that little bit of change, I mean that's if you want to look at it like that. But the way I see it , I'm out here risking it all so that my son can have a better place he could call home.

When I walk in my house and I see him at the table eating dinner in peace," he continued, "I know he's at peace because I'm out here putting in work. When I see him smile because of his good efforts in school, that's when I see what I'm doing out here is worth it. My point of saying all that is, we have to look beyond all the things that won't matter in the next few months and play for the future."

He paused for a moment and walked over to the desk that sat in front of the conference room and stated, "So when I'm out here risking my life to keep drugs off the streets, I don't look at how much I'm making on my check, I look at the effect I'm making in the streets! So for future references, be true to what you believe in, whether it's good or bad. But do remember what is done in the dark always surfaces to the light!"

Without speaking another word Honeycutt walked out of the conference room and headed straight to the parking lot with his team only paces behind him.

****

Black, Hamburger, Big Ox and Rip sat in the middle room of 1122 playing *NBA Live* with a blunt rotating between them, while Butler was at the front door with the cage locked. They all was waiting on Kruger who had just called and said that he was on his way.

It was actually five after four when Butler spotted the four unmarked cars turn on Summer Street off of Laney-Walker Boulevard, one behind the other. He quickly slammed the wood door shut and secured it with the two by four wedge. Seconds later he was running down the hall towards the middle room.

"Man what the fuck is up with you?" Big Ox asked after he stepped through the door.

"Them folks just pulled up and it looks like they're coming in," he responded as he tried to catch his breath.

It took the fellas a half a second to react to what they were just told. They all moved with the determination of Micheal Jordan in the fourth quarter as they dropped their guns, dope and scales through the drop holes around the house.

"How many cars?" Hamburger asked him.

"I really don't know," Butler answered.

"Well, you can go and open the door if you wanna," Black implied.

"Say what?!" Rip questioned with a confused expression.

"Man, chill out and let Butler go and open the door," Black replied with a light smile, "we ain't got shit in here right now and all they gonna do is yank the gate off and that'll cost more than anything."

After a few moments Hamburger agreed, "Yeah Butler, open the door before they snatch the gate off."

Butler went and did as he was told. When he opened the door the agents was hooking some type of device to the gate to open it.

"Man, what the hell are ya'll doing?" Butler stressed with a light smile as he opened the door and gate.

"Get your ass on the ground right now!" One of the agents demanded with his pistol pointed at Butler's chest.

Butler instantly complied in the middle of the hallway, while six agents speeded pass him and up the hall with their pistols drawn.

After checking the first two rooms and seeing that there wasn't any occupants, they made their way down the hall towards the middle room.

"Get ya'll ass on the floor now!" The first of the six stated as they filled the middle room.

"Man, ya'll go ahead and handle ya'll business," Black stated with his eyes on the TV screen, "I have money on this game."

"I think my partner told you to get your ass on the floor!" An agent stated after pulling the plug out of the wall.

"Man you don't even have to go there!" Big Ox stressed.

"Don't let me have to tell you to hit the floor again!" The first agent stated as beads of sweat appeared on his forehead.

"Lets get on the floor fellas," Hamburger stressed, "I don't need to be catching a slug from one of these suckas."

Twenty minutes later the fellas were waving good-bye to Honeycutt and his crew from the porch.

A large crowd had accumulated across the street and among them was Kruger. He'd noticed Sanchez and Olgetree getting inside the blue Jimmy truck, along with another agent. After they made eye contact, Kruger gave them a cold stare.

Kruger was so heated about them not notifying him that he didn't have the patience to wait until they all left the premises before he walked across the street. When Honeycutt noticed who he was, he stepped back over to the porch.

"You must have left something?" Rip asked him.

"I just wanted to have a word with Mr. Pearsey," he replied with his eyes focused on Kruger.

"Now, why would you go out of your way to speak with me?" Kruger asked with a sly grin before adding, "you only do that sort of thing with friends."

Honeycutt just smirked as if he knew something that Kruger didn't, before he replied, "I just wanted you to know that your run is just about up."

All the fellas watched as Honeycutt made his way back to his vehicle before Rip stressed, "Playboy, it sounds as if he done made this thing personal."

"See that's where we've been slipping at," Kruger replied after taking a seat on the porch.

"What's that my folk?" Black asked.

"With Honeycutt, it's always been personal."

-TERESA-

"NOW WHEN A WOMAN'S FED UP, THERE'S NOTHING YOU CAN DO ABOUT IT!" Is what R-Kelly was humming in my ear.

He knows that he stay bringing that fire to the table. I can feel him all the way on this one, or at least he can feel me.

STILL STUCK

Toya just left from over her with all her little jokes and things. Here it is Halloween and she joking around about taking me trick or treating because I look like a mummy with this cast on. She just don't know how much I was considering her offer.

Lord knows that I'm about to lose my mind if I stay in this apartment the way I've been doing, but who wants to model a cast. I still have a couple of weeks with this thing, and after they cut it off, I still have to go through therapy.

Deamon says he'll go with me, but I don't think that's a good idea, not with us trying to back out of this relationship. He still keeps stressing the fact that we're still friends, which is true, but he still has to give me some time to marinate on our separation. This shit ain't easy!

I just had a dream about my baby. It's like I can hear him calling me. It feels as if I'm running to the sound of him crying for hours, but we never come in contact and I never see his face.

I'm thinking about taking my ass back to school and leave this prison business alone, that's not really my style. I feel where Deamon was coming from when he said that it was like I left my dreams alone. I mean, when I think about it

I'm tired of walking through those wire fences and wearing that silly ass uniform. That shit is for a muthafuckas who has already lived or has no passion to live.

"Hey Teresa, you need anything?" Tamika is asking at my bedroom door.

"Girl, I need to be asking you that," I replied with a light giggle before I crawled out of bed.

"You know I'm alright, I'm just trying to stay active so my baby won't be all lazy."

I know she doesn't mean any harm by the comment, and I don't wish any bad luck on her or anything, but I kind of feel a little envious.

"Your mama told you that too, huh?" I replied with a sly grin.

"Yeah," she stated in a nonchalant manner as if she read my thoughts.

"Well, if I was you I'd listen to her, cause she done had five of ya'll," I stated as I walked towards the bathroom before asking, "Have you heard from your brother?"

"Yeah, he running around somewhere," she replied as she leaned against the bathroom door.

"Isn't Slanga suppose to go to court today?" I asked.

"No that's next Friday," she replied before adding, "I don't know if they gonna let him out though, you know they put that boy in the trunk."

"Yeah, I heard," I replied after washing my face before asking her, "do you think your brother had something to do with that?"

"Nine times out of ten," she replied with a devious grin, "that nigga like shit like that."

"Well, he better slow his ass down, cause he can't thug all his life!" I stressed with concern.

"I bet you can't tell him that," she replied with a smirk as she went up the hall.

If you ask me, she's just as crazy as him.

****

__Good morning__ Mr Singleton," Kruger stated as he walked into his office.

"How you doing Mr. Pearsey, is there anything new you need to inform me about?" He replied with a friendly smile.

"Na'll, everything is pretty much the same as last month, but call my girl a little later," he replied as he took a seat.

"Well, I need you to be aware that you might be changing parole officers in the near future," he stated as if it was nothing but protocol.

Kruger obviously didn't feel the same way because he spatted out, "And why is that?!"

"Because there is a lot of controversy about our relationship in this office."

"What type controversy? Hell, what relationship?!" He stressed, " I'm the parolee and you're the parole officer, it's as simple as that!"

"I'm very aware of that, but there was a Detective Honeycutt who called here last week feeding us information about you being a part of some type of drug cartel."

"Say what?!"

"Now my boss wants to put a heavier watch on you, I mean give you like a nine o'clock curfew and all."

"Well, why you just telling me?"

"Because I thought he was just bluffing, until I came in this morning and he gave me these curfew papers for you."'

"All of this behind some he say she say shit?!"

"Calm down Mr. Pearsey, we can work around this," he stated in an assuring manner, "but you have to make sure you be at your house at nine tonight."

"If it ain't one thing, it's another," he spat out as he raised from his seat.

"Make sure you be at the house at nine, because I feel that my boss is gonna ride with me, he's really hung up about this."

"Well, I'll be at the house," he stated as he dropped his supervision fee on the table.

"Well talk about it later on tonight, but I do believe that we have it all under control," he replied with an assuring smile.

"I hope so Mr. Singleton, I really hope so."

-KRUGER-

I don't think that people really know how hard it is to be coming in the house at nine o'clock every night. It doesn't have to be like that, but Singleton's so called boss has been coming through here every hour on the hour, until Deidra tells him that I'm sleep.

The thing that really irks me is I can't handle my business at night, like I've grown accustomed to, so it's really been hell for a hustler. The only thing I really have to look forward to is Slanga's preliminary hearing tomorrow.

Amanda ass is all balled up on the couch talking to him on the phone. He should come through with flying colors though, so he good.

"Kruger, my boo wants to talk to you," I hear her say as she raises from the couch and makes her way toward the kitchen table to hand me the phone.

"What up big homie?" I stated after finishing my glass of *Hennessy*.

"Tomorrow playboy," I heard him say.

"I can definitely feel that, cause I know you ready to jump that ship."

"You know it like a poet playboy!" He stressed with authority before adding, "My lawyer came through earlier and said that I should be back on the streets by tomorrow afternoon. He say that nigga Buck is gonna testify on my behalf."

"Well, at least we know that money really does make the world go round."

"True that, but you know that you can't come to court tomorrow, just be on call until I get out."

"I wasn't planning on coming anyway," I responded as I poured me another drink, "Ole boy might start having flash backs and point me out or some shit like that."

"That's just how I was thinking. You know we can't be too sure about nothing when dealing with snakes and leeches."

"You know I know, that's why I keep my grass cut, and far from that swamp water."

This caused him to chuckle a little, which was good, cause all week he'd been sounding depressed.

"I guess I'll see you tomorrow bra," he stated.

"For sure."

"Much love!"

"Til death, playboy!" I replied right before I passed Amanda back the phone.

Now Deidra is standing over me with a plate full of lasagna and broccoli and cheese. I mean you have to love this woman. After she handed me the plate she sat next to me at the table.

"Preciate this baby girl," I said as I kissed her on the forehead.

She just smiled before saying, "Much love playboy!"

I couldn't help but burst out laughing because I knew that she was mocking me and Slanga.

"Til death beautiful," I managed to utter out after regaining my composure.

After all the bullshit, I still have someone I lay next to at night that I can laugh and joke with. I guess you can say that she makes me feel at ease at my most tense moments.

****

The courtroom was half empty and the only people that Deidra and Amanda recognized in the room was Gunslanga's two lawyers. There was this black guy who wore a patch over his eye that sat just four rows in front of them, who both woman took to be Gunslanga's alleged victim.

He sat by an older woman who looked as if she wore her Sunday dress with the matching hat. Only a fool wouldn't realize that she was the victim's mother. The shirt and tie the alleged victim wore was sort of awkward. His shirt had the look as if it was originally owed by someone who was a lot bigger than he was, because the collar had at least a two inch gap from his neck.

The judge had just asked for Gunslanga and the bailiff was headed to the holding area to retrieve him.

When Gunslanga stepped in the courtroom, Amanda noticed that his hair desperately needed to be braided. The whole courtroom noticed how his alleged victim started shivering as if the grim reaper had just walked in.

After looking over at the district attorney, Deidra realized that she was the same white woman who was over her last assault and battery case.

Suzanne Hicks wanted so badly to convict Deidra on the case that she ended up indicting her on the wrong charges, so the state had to drop the charges all together. Mrs. Hicks hated the fact that Deidra never did time, despite her violent history. It pissed her off that Deidra caught a smooth ride because of her father's status. Now that was something no-one dared to mentioned in public, but Mrs. Hicks went so far as to mention it in the courtroom.

"Your honor," Mrs. Hicks started to say, "here is the case of the state of Georgia vs Robert Frazier, on the charges of kidnapping, aggravated assault and assault with a deadly weapon."

"Does the state have its witness present?" The judge asked.

Gunslanga turned around to look at Amanda and Deidra before he glared over at his alleged victim.

"Yes your honor, the state has all its witnesses present at the time," Mrs. Hicks answered.

"Well, get on with it," the judge responded in an impatient manner.

"Sir, the state calls Bobby Ferguson to the stand."

The eye patched guy stood up and made his way towards the witness stand. Before he sat down, he was forced to raise his left hand and place his right on the bible.

"Now do you solemnly swear to tell the truth, nothing but the truth so help you GOD?" The bailiff asked him.

"I do," he replied in a nervous manner as if he was on trial for his own life.

"Your witness Mrs. Hicks," the judge stated.

"Thank you, your honor," she responded without looking up at him as she fumbled through some papers, before asking, "Now Mr. Ferguson, do you know Mr. Frazier?"

"Yes," he weakly replied.

"How do you know him?" She asked as she walked closer to the stand.

"He tried to help me the night I got jumped," he stuttered out before adding, "I tried to tell the officers the truth, but they seemed to want him locked up so bad that they created their own story."

"Say what?!" Mrs. Hicks responded openly flushed by the statement.

"Yes mamm," he quickly responded, "Mr. Frazier is the one who took me to the hospital, if it wasn't for him I probably wouldn't be here today."

"You mean to tell me that the defendant is actually your savior in this matter?" The judge asked in a confused manner.

"I wouldn't say my savior, because Jesus Christ is my savior, but he was my hero," he replied with a smile.

The judge then looked over at Ms. Hicks and asked, "Can you please tell me why I'm wasting precious court time on this case. I have you know that I order all of these charges dismissed immediately and I need to see you in my chambers," he stated with a disgruntled expression.

As the mallet slammed against the judge desk, Gunslanga winked his eye at his alleged victim.

****

Lieutenant Honeycutt sat behind his desk going through a few files when his cell phone rung.

"Honeycutt," he stated after answering.

"I need some attention," the female voice implied.

Honeycutt rarely smiled, but after hearing her voice he wore a huge one.

"Hello, and how are you doing?" He replied in a modest tone.

"Not so good," she replied in an agitated manner before adding, "I just had a case in the municipal building and you won't believe how it collapsed on me."

"What kind of case?"

"Kidnapping and aggravated assault."

"Who was the defendant?"

"A Robert Frazier, have you heard of him?"

"Yes, I've known him for quite some time," he replied, "I busted him a few years back on drug charges. He did a few years on it, but now he's out and right back to doing the same thing."

"What's the purpose of us locking them up if they're just going to keep setting them free?!"

"I wish you would have got at me about him before, I'm sure we could've built a case against him," Honeycutt firmly stated.

"Is that so?" She asked in a surprised manner.

"What are you conjuring up Suzanne?" He asked as if he knew she was up to something.

"I have a good idea why my case fell the way it did. In court today I saw a young lady, who's father just happens to be the lead homicide detective."

"Are you talking about O'Neil's chap?"

"Yes Deidra O'Neil, I think maybe she's Frazier's girlfriend."

"And?"

"And, if that's so, then that's how we take them down."

"I don't understand," he replied in a confused manner.

385

"I don't know about you Mark, but I want this son of a bitch off the streets. He's the prime example of the scum of the earth, and with O'Neil's daughter by his side, he may feel as if he's above the law."

"Let me say this," he stated before taking a deep breath and adding, "following O'Neil's daughter around isn't gonna get us nowhere. Robert is smarter than you think and he's not alone. If you want, I don't mind showing you his crew. They're all in it together, but his main partner is Deamon Pearsey."

"Well, I'll call you in an half of hour with the room number, because I still need some attention."

His rare smile appeared again before he replied with, "I'll bring a bottle."

"Mark, come prepared to fuck!" She stated with an attitude before adding, "You can make love to your wife later."

"Crazy bitch!" He managed to utter out with a sly grin after hanging the phone up.